THE LURE OF BOATING
(a cautionary tale)

Howard S. Selden

W & B Publishers
USA

W & B Publishers

For information:
W & B Publishers
Post Office Box 193
Colfax, NC 27235
www.a-argusbooks.com

ISBN: 9781942981190
ISBN: 1942981198

Book Cover designed by Dubya
Printed in the United States of America

A Dedication Ode

I looked so much like him I could have been his son or brother, though I was his nephew.

It has been said not to mourn sufficiently is to mourn forever. The unrelenting sorrow is a wound that never heals. It lurks below the surface coloring thoughts and depressing joy. I have experienced such pain. It's like some chronic disease.

The eyes, oh the eyes look at me. They cut deeply into my soul, opening memories only thinly scabbed. Can a baby's eyes speak from a picture of long ago? I say yes, for the eyes are the same as the man's. They are without fear or regret, yet seem to grasp that life will offer pain and anguish. I am haunted and nourished by those eyes: they speak volumes of past times and futures never lived. The fullness of his life was only a begrudged twenty-nine seasons.

There is no salve for pain of his never knowing. Knowing how well I bloomed.

The fire in my belly to prove my worth still smolders, since he is not here to nod his approval with those calm, unblinking eyes.

I lived in his shadow, and relished the role. He beckoned me into his world and spoke of grown-up matters. Never a lecture, only quiet thoughts of values, and about his life's awesome dependency on insulin. How speechless and stunned I was to hear him quietly tell how he didn't expect a long life.

I can still hear the sound of his melodious bass singing voice, delighting the dreamy-eyed old-timers with Yiddish songs of long ago. They adored him for it, while I sat silently, both proud and jealous at the same time.

How I hunger for his hand on my shoulder and the embrace of unconditional love.

Also

By Howard S. Selden

Science Fiction

The Pariah Stigma

Memoir

A Dental Odyssey [unlikely musings of a dentist]

Novels

The Shaman and the Jew

Wapasha and the Rabbi

An Unusual Encounter

The Skier

CHAPTER ONE

Lou was fascinated with boating. It wasn't as though he came from a boating family, or had relatives or friends who had expressed an interest or longed to be involved. When asked, he couldn't readily explain why.

The only remote reference to boats was from his father, Joe, who on rare occasion when urged, would tell of his terrible sea voyage to America. His story began in Russia.

“I received first class steamship tickets for myself and my oldest sister, sent by my father, Sam, from America. As the oldest of five boys—in my early teens—along with my sister, we understood it was our turn to join our father. Our earnings were needed to eventually be able to buy tickets for my mother and the six other children. In the meantime, the family would have to wait in Russia for better times. We were thrilled at the prospects of the trip and our new life in America.

"But what has bothered me all these years has been the foolishness for the extravagant purchase of first class berths, considering my father's dire impoverished status at the time. The details are vague, but it seemed that an unscrupulous salesman who preyed on his naive fellow *lantsleit* ("countrymen), had arranged the sale. Sam was among the masses of recent immigrant men, who struggled for meager livings in a new country with its intimidating and very confusing language, while families remained in the old country. He had trusted the Yiddish speaking salesman for guidance. Instead he was ill-advised and sold more expensive tickets than he could afford or needed. I recall how my father scrimped and saved to make the weekly payments, which took many years to clear the debt."

Joe always paused at this point. He was moved by his recollections, and needed a moment to compose himself. Occasionally, he was so distracted as to forget his wife's protests about those 'awful smelling things,' and lit up a cigar, which normally he would obediently smoke outside.

Finally he picked up the thread of the story again.

"I was all excited about the trip on a large ocean liner. My life had been entirely centered around our *Shtetl* ("small village"), which as a matter of fact I had never previously left, and I knew nothing of the outside world. So on the way to the port I was overwhelmed by everything we encountered. Probably my most important discovery was ice cream. Don't laugh! I never heard of ice cream before, but after one taste I fell in love with it. You know that it's still my favorite treat to this day.

"But my expectations were shattered as soon as I boarded the ship: I immediately became very seasick—and remained totally prostrated with it for the entire voyage. It was the most awful experience of my life. All I could do was lie in my bunk, fearful of dying while at the same time wishing I would, never able to enjoy my deluxe surroundings, nor eat any of the elegant food provided for first-class passengers. Just talking about that boat trip is enough to make me queasy."

And finally to underscore the basic troubling issue, Joe invariably invoked a Yiddish expression for emphasis, "Buying those expensive first class tickets was *aroysgevorfen gelt* ("thrown-out money")."

Some years later, when he owned a large powerboat, Lou had an exchange one day with a friend, and was asked, "Why do you want to buy a new boat, when you already have such an impressive one?" Lou smiled and answered without hesitation, "You don't understand. I absolutely lust for it." Lou had chosen the word lust because it accurately expressed his longing . He thought to himself, *There's no doubt, but I am in a fever pitch of anticipation about this new boat, and the word lust feels just right. It aptly describes my emotional state. I realize I'm sort of caught in a manic-like web, in which I perversely relish the high pitched arousal. Nonetheless, I am determined to buy a bigger boat, despite the possible pitfalls."* The 'lust' lasted a number of years, which led to the acquisition of increasingly bigger boats . . . before the fever burned out.

***

Looking back, Lou was keenly aware when he first knew that he was captivated with boats. It began when he agreed to join Jay, a college friend, on a canoe trip during the forthcoming summer.

Little did Jay realize at the time that he would be instrumental in initiating Lou's passionate boating involvement. Jay somehow knew all about the logistics involved: Lake George up in the Adirondack Mountains of New York State was the place to go; a canoe and camping gear could be rented at Bolton Landing Cove on the lake; they would paddle to one of the many small islands and camp out for a week; and for the essential transportation, Jay could borrow his uncle's car.

***

It was late afternoon when they pushed off from the Cove, with the canoe overloaded with camping equipment, groceries, and duffle bags filled with their personal stuff.

Since Lou had considerable experience canoeing as a boy scout, he kneeled in the stern with steering responsibility. After smoothly paddling out of Bolton Cove, thrilled with the prospects of the ongoing adventure, they entered the wide lake. Without warning the surface of the water abruptly changed. Suddenly they were confronted with waves over two feet in height which crashed over the bow, one after the other. Their situation quickly became critical. Joy had rapidly vanished, to be replaced by fear.

Despite vigorous paddling, they soon realized they weren't making any headway against the waves and strong wind. Furthermore, the boat was filling with water. Lou recognized they were in danger and shouted to Jay, "We'll never make it to the island. We must immediately turn back."

It was already too late. Before they could turn the canoe around, the water-filled boat started to sink. Lou knew how to swim, but his clothing weighed him down. While trying to pull off the clinging, water-logged, heavy, wool sweater it became tangled in his undershirt. In desperation he struggled to free himself, as he sank ever deeper under the water. The claustrophobic entanglement with the clothing and fear of drowning energized an extremely strenuous effort. He tore frantically at the garments with all his might. In those fleeting seconds he knew his life hung in the balance, as his lungs screamed for air. Sensing his awful plight, he marshaled an hysterical effort, and abruptly the sweater and undershirt slipped over his head. At once he furiously surged towards the surface, which during the hectic struggle had faded far overhead. Just as he felt his lungs would burst, he broke through into the air and gasped and gulped deeply. It would be an understatement to simply say Lou was overwhelmed with relief. The shock of coming so close to drowning had terrified him. His teeth were chattering and he uncontrollably shivered in the warm lake water. Slowly he calmed down, and soon his breathing became fairly regular.

Everything had happened rapidly, and the serious totality of the situation was slow to clarify. Confused for a while, he instinctively treaded water and vaguely speculated, *Could I swim to the island off in the distance?* When he looked around and found Jay treading water only a few feet away, he first felt relieved, then was shocked to realize that he had completely forgotten about him.

To his surprise, the canoe was floating nearby deeply settled into the water up to its gunwales, with many of their various possessions drifting around. The lake looked empty and Lou wondered, *Where had all the other boats gone?* Then as if summoned to save them, he spotted a small boat coming their way, from out on the lake.

An older fisherman and a youngster were speeding back to Bolton Cove. Their outing was likely cut short when the water turned dangerous. As the small boat drew near, with the boys frantically waving, they were spotted. Gratefully the outboard motor slowed and approached closely. The old-timer's voice was anxious and impatient as he called out, "Come on and quickly climb in, but don't bring any of your stuff. The boat can't hold much more." Jay and Lou swam over to him, and ignored his protests as they each urgently grabbed a floating duffle and dragged it into the boat. Without the precious duffels they would have lost everything: extra clothing and their wallets which were also stored in there.

The man grumbled and shook his head, but headed for shore. He probably saved their lives and soon landed them safely.

Lou and Jay tried vainly to express their appreciation, but never got a chance. After silently tying up the boat, he and the boy left quickly, without so much as a farewell nod. His inexplicable sullen demeanor left Lou and Jay feeling bewildered. The impact of what occurred and their dire circumstances slowly sank in. After standing immobilized, dripping wet and chilled in only their undershorts and sodden sneakers for a few moments, they shrugged off their indecision and sprang into action. Youthful energy and optimism served them well.

They opened their tightly closed duffle bags and dug out fresh clothes, and were surprised that they were only slightly damp. Sadly, Jay's prized expensive camera, which he hadn't stored, had been lost in the lake, but he was delighted to find the car keys in the duffle where he had put them. At least they had the car and most of their personal belongings. The canoe and some of the floatable gear would have to be salvaged by the rental firm.

Before they left, they reported the accident at the rental office. The agent listened calmly, and nonchalantly told them how lucky they were to be alive, since many people drowned in the lake each year. For good measure he added, "The lake looks calm and peaceful, but strangers don't know how quickly it changes. It's like some evil spirit takes over and enjoys frightening people and then drowning some."

Despite the harrowing experience, and maybe because of it, Lou knew that he was forever drawn to boating.

CHAPTER TWO

When Lou's near-drowning experience on Lake George is coupled with his memories of almost drowning in a river at the age of five, it's surprising that he nevertheless remained attracted to boating. Perhaps his elemental fear of the water was paradoxically offset by a fascination with boats. In all likely-hood, the mixture of heightened excitement and elevated anxiety combined to create an irresistible emotional mix. He eagerly threw himself into the nautical world. Small sailboats on small lakes were initially absorbing, but by and by when his interest lagged he turned his focus to powerboats. He imagined long cruises, even out onto the deep ocean with visits to coastal ports of call. Also, the challenge of mastering the handling of diverse types of boats had a tantalizing appeal. The thought of all the new things he would have to learn was stimulating and exciting. He couldn't wait.

***

Lou started with a sailboat: a twelve foot fiberglass O'Day, called a Widgeon. The single mast was rigged with a mainsail and spinnaker (a large triangular sail running from the bow to the mast) and a retractable centerboard (keel). For his first season Lou sailed on the convenient local lakes, and was able to learn the basics of sailboat handling.

But, as anticipated, it didn't take long for 'lust' to manifest itself, and the following year Lou traded the Widgeon. The new boat was called a Day Sailor, with a configuration similar to that of the Widgeon, only larger. It had an overall length of sixteen feet nine inches, and was the most popular sailboat ever produced. Since its first availability in 1959, over thirteen thousand were reported sold. In addition to a roomier cockpit the Day Sailor had a spacious cuddy cabin in the bow—a variable use space for storage, just big enough for an average-sized adult to crawl into.

For a few seasons the sailing satisfied Lou, but eventually he grew restless and decided to make a dramatic change: He would switch to a powerboat, and seek out more 'consequential' waters.

***

Lou followed his gut reactions, and thought, *With a powerboat I'll travel and explore as the whim dictated and not be dependent on the wind. I know my sailboat friends were appalled at my decision to sell my sailboat and buy a powerboat. Hoping to raise my ire they gleefully ridiculed my intentions by referring to it as a 'stink-pot.' But to hell with them.*

Stirred to action, Lou wasted no time. He impulsively purchased a new twenty-foot, single engine I/O, with a small cabin, galley, head, and accommodations to sleep four. On eventual reflection, Lou was incredulous that it had never entered his mind to find a slip for the boat before buying it. He was so caught up in the excitement of the moment that it totally blocked other thoughts, even the obvious. Impossible as it sounds, that is what happened. He planned to berth the boat on the Hudson River, and the reasonable thing to have done was at least to initially survey possible locations, and available marinas. His subsequent frustration was predictable.

However, Lou quickly learned how totally ignorant he was about power boats, but to his credit he soaked up the new information like a sponge. He learned the I/O stood for inboard/outboard marine propulsion system, innovated by Volvo and introduced in 1959. The I/O combined the features and advantages of an inboard engine with the flexibility of an outboard motor. In straight inboard configurations the engine is located in the central bilge area of the boat, with power transmitted through a spinning drive shaft (called the screw) to the fixed position propeller, which rotates either clockwise or counterclockwise. In a single-screw straight inboard, when going forward, with the prop turning clockwise, there is a tendency for the boat to slightly drift to the starboard (the right side while looking forward). Only a minor steering correction with the rudder is needed to compensate.

On the other hand, when running the engine in reverse the propeller spins counterclockwise, and steering limitations can develop. Backing the boat calls for more complex skills by the helmsman: judicious use of the rudder position coordinated with timely use of engine power are required. The single engine I/O overcame these problems and steering was made easier.

Popular outboard engines, commonly used on small to moderately-sized boats, are attached over the center of the stern and suspended into the water. Integrated into the unit are both powerhead and propeller. The outboard's swiveling capability enables sharper turns going forward, and the ability to run backwards to port as well as starboard. The disadvantage of placing all the motor's weight on the back of the boat is the tendency to unbalance the vessel by tipping the bow up.

Volvo cleverly created the I/O hybrid by separating the powerhead from the outboard's bottom half with its propeller housing. The engine was placed in the bottom of the boat (as with inboard engines); and the propeller remained over the stern. But, since the I/O contains only the lighter propeller assembly – unlike regular outboards – it's considerably lighter. Therefore, the I/O more effectively balanced the vessel's trim; enabled increased inboard engine size and power; and with the advantages of the outdrive's swiveling ability steering was dramatically improved— and accomplished without rudder help at idle speed. In addition, the novel I/O arrangement provided improved access for repairs.

***

Now that Lou owned a boat, he urgently had to find a berth in a marina. Since the boat had been locally purchased in Eastern Pennsylvania, he decided that the Hudson River would be convenient. From there he imagined cruises out to Long Island Sound, and beyond. So, on the first available Sunday after the purchase, he headed for the river, naively expecting to easily find a berth. He was rudely shocked to discover that marinas were few in number and open berths were nonexistent. The disappointing search began on the New Jersey side of the Hudson at the base of the George Washington Bridge, and continued north. By late afternoon he felt fatigued, and decidedly depressed. He just could not find a place for his boat. After crossing the border into New York State he stopped in the town of Nyack, where he was directed to Peterson's Boatyard in North

Nyack. Somewhat reluctantly, he approached Peterson's.

This'll be my last frustrating inquiry, he thought to himself. Looking at the large building, set back from the river, with a modest network of docks in which a few decrepit boats were tied up, he observed, *This place doesn't even look like a real marina. It's old, badly weathered and run-down, and appears deserted.* To his surprise, he found the front door open.

Having come this far, he entered, figuring, *I might as well look around.* Even though a nautical novice, he recognized that the large room contained a wide display of supplies needed by boat owners. It was an impressive marine supply store. Like most men, Lou loved hardware stores, and couldn't resist examining and marveling at all the shiny and cleverly designed items. As he looked around, he concluded, *Wow, am I going to enjoy this boat business. Just look at all these wondrous things. What fun it'll be to learn their use.*

He stood still, a little confused, not certain what to do, and baffled as to why nobody was around. Before he turned to leave he noticed an open door at the extreme end of the room, and decided to walk over for a look. To his astonishment, he found a well dressed elderly gentleman sitting at a desk in a small cluttered office. Lou hesitated, then said, "Excuse me, Mr. Peterson. I'm looking for a berth for my power boat, and since your door was open I thought I'd come in and inquire whether you had any space available."

The man smiled and told Lou, "My name isn't Peterson. He's long gone. My name is Carl, and I'm the manager of the Boatyard." Without any preamble Mr. Carl launched into an account of how this yard helped win World War II. He proudly recalled, "Why, young fellow, we built those fast P-T boasts right here, made famous by President Kennedy's service on one. See those photos on the walls. Start on the left and they depict ships in progressive stages of construction. Yes, sir, there weren't many yards like us with as many skilled men who knew how to work wood. Of course, those were the days before fiberglass." Mr. Carl's eyes sparkled, he seemed to sit up straighter, and his cheeks glowed with a faint pleasurable pink.

Lou was totally impressed with Carl's spontaneous monologue and thought to himself, *Those were memorable years, both in the country's and the yard's history, which likely were the high point in Carl's life. Understandably, he was nourished by keeping those recollections alive.*

Lou was quiet, listened politely, couldn't help but sense Mr. Carl's regrets, and reflected, *He is at the end of his days. Like the Boatyard, in which he clearly identified, their glorious times were over, never to be lived again. Those purposeful days, fueled with the call of destiny which energized a generation had faded.* The distraction of the moment left Lou lost in reverie. He wondered, *Will I too have a halcyon moment or special interval to recall in my old age?*

He was startled when Mr. Carl returned to the question of available slips. "Now I know that our slips here at the Boatyard are all committed. But let me call the Tarrytown Boat Club, directly across the river, and see what they have to say." With that he immediately dialed and spoke to the Tarrytown dock-master, but they were also filled. Lou expressed his appreciation, turned to go, with disappointment clearly evident in the tone of his voice. Mr. Carl, perhaps noted Lou's sad mood, called out, "You know, I really don't handle rental of berths. On Monday you should call my secretary. Maybe she could help." Then he made a hasty search for a piece of paper among the jumble of documents and catalogues on his desk. Finally he tore off the blank bottom of a letter, on which he wrote her name and phone number. Lou put the note in his pocket, and was moved by Carl's persistence and generosity of spirit. He thanked him again for his time and help, and left with a heavy heart. It was a sad day, filled with a sense of rejection and failure.

***

Late Monday morning, while anticipating another negative response, Lou nevertheless called Peterson's. Instead he was greeted by a cheerful woman who said, "Mr. Carl told me to expect your call. It so happened that one of the slips in the Lower Yard has become available, but will accommodate boats only up to twenty feet in length." Without any idea where or what was the Lower Yard, or its cost, calmly as possible, Lou said, "My boat will fit, and I'm delighted to take it." He could have jumped with joy, and mumbled, *Good old Mr. Carl. He came through like he said he would.*

***

In revived high spirits, Lou now moved to arrange the logistics of getting the boat to the Hudson River. First order of business, Lou decided, was to check with the local dealer in order to coordinate the delivery of the boat with Peterson's. The dealer was more than cooperative, and offered his services when convenient with the Boatyard.

In the meantime, Lou knew that the propeller was being changed for an upgraded larger one—the dealer's decision—at no additional cost. Everything was moving along smoothly. Impatient to hasten progress, Lou went to see the boat, and just happened to arrive as a young mechanic was fitting the new propeller onto the outdrive of his I/O. Lou watched as he finished. He took particular notice how the outdrive's sheet metal cover was fastened in place with a few screws. This chance encounter would subsequently prove to be incredibly useful to Lou. It was a moment charged with serendipity.

Next, he called Peterson's to arrange the boat's launching. With his mind racing ahead, he wondered how a launching was managed. So, while on the phone he couldn't resist asking, "By the way, how is that accomplished?" Rather matter-of-factly he was told, "It's done with a travel lift." It was a new term to Lou, among the many he would learn, so he simply answered, "Swell. I'll see you soon." Though this was all new to him, he tried not to sound too uninformed. He observed to himself, *I'll learn all about the travel lift when I sees it in action.* As he hoped, every step in boating was indeed stimulating.

On the big day for launching, Lou's car led the truck carrying the boat to Peterson's, and they arrived on schedule. Waiting for them in the parking area was a huge ungainly device which Lou rightly concluded, *That had to be the travel lift.* He learned it was a self-propelled marine transporter, commonly found in boat service facilities.

Without discussion, much like a well-rehearsed ballet, the truck driver and travel lift operator synchronized the movements of their respective vehicles: the truck backed into the correct location; then the noisy, lumbering travel lift moved over the truck, and straddled the flatbed on which the boat was secured. Two thick slings (constructed of a heavy-duty nylon material) were looped under the boat. It was obvious even to Lou, that their placement were critical. If the slings were ineptly positioned, a disastrous accident could occur as the boat was lifted: It could tip, slide off the slings, and crash to the ground. Lou nervously held his breath as the process began, and smiled with relief as the boat was masterfully lifted up. Once the boat was clear of the truck, the driver promptly drove off on his trip back to Pennsylvania. With the well-balanced boat cradled securely in the slings, the travel lift moved onto ramps which extended out over the water, and gently lowered the boat onto the river, without so much as a single splash. The entire impressive process took only a few minutes.

***

What started smoothly was soon to change, and would be an harbinger of what future boating experiences might entail. Lou climbed down into the boat full of joy and excitement. At last, this was the day he impatiently looked forward to. He was charged with visions of cruising on the mighty Hudson River, with trips out to Long Island Sound, and even beyond onto the Atlantic Ocean. The excitement bordered on nervousness, but he felt confident he could handle the boat. After all, he figured, *the controls are simple and it's like driving a car, only on water.*

A dissonant intrusion presented itself when he found that the boat's bow was pointed towards the land, and not towards the river. For his maiden voyage he expected a straight run out of the yard. He looked around to see if there was enough room to turn the boat around, but the space was too narrow. Reluctantly, Lou had no choice but to simply back out, a maneuver he had hoped to avoid. Furthermore, the yard crew were quietly watching, which increased his tension. So, trying to look calm like he had done this many times, he shifted into reverse and slowly and cautiously backed out. Mumbling to himself he said, *That wasn't too bad. I think I managed it quite well. Now I'll simply turn the stern upstream in preparation for the downstream run. After all it's only about a mile to the Lower Yard, where my wife is waiting to welcome my arrival and help tie-up the boat.*

But, to his shock and alarm, when he tried to shift into forward gear the lever refused to move. The boat was now adrift in the river's swift tidal ebb current (flowing out to sea), unsettling Lou to the near edge of panic. In a moment's time, his exuberance and confidence had been replaced with fear. Incredulously his continuing efforts to move the shift lever failed. Lou couldn't help but envision an unfolding catastrophe. He was alone, without any hope of assistance. An acute sense of helplessness threatened to overwhelm him.

At the same time, the pressure of the looming crisis had also provoked an instinctive positive response: All his senses were keenly awakened. It was a pure 'fight or flight' physiologic response, with blood and nutrition rapidly shunted to his muscles. With desperate white knuckles his left hand's grip on the steering wheel hadn't weakened, but reflexively tightened. Furthermore, despite the fog of disorientation and emotional turmoil, he knew to steer as best he could to keep the bow pointed downstream, and out in the river safely away from the shallows or any hazardous objects along the river bank.

Finally, despair fueled with anger—at the dealer's negligence to properly service the boat—Lou marshaled all his strength and with both hands he frantically pulled on the shift lever, thinking, *I'll move it or break it. It's do or die.*

With a sudden jolt the gear moved into forward position, almost causing Lou to lose balance. The engagement of the gears signaled that he had blessedly prevailed: He had gained control of the boat. Lou breathed easily again, and sighed mightily with relief. But the tension had its impact. With the crisis over, he became aware of uncomfortable stomach cramps, which would plague him during years of boating. He ignored these bouts, didn't tell his wife Nicole about them, and figured it was the price he paid for boating.

Nicole waved a joyous greeting as his boat cautiously entered the Lower Yard. Her misgivings about this entire boating situation had been the cause of some considerable controversy, and with reluctance she had agreed to participate. Yet, her sense of relief to see Lou safely arrive counterbalanced her frustration, at least for the moment. Though his persistence in buying the boat would continue to wrangle.

Lou's dark visage was obvious to Nicole, who as usual could 'read him like a book.' Concerned she called out, "What's the trouble, Lou? You look like you're ready to kill." Lou didn't answer as he angrily banged the shift lever forcefully in and out of forward and reverse gears, in order to tease the boat into the small slip. With suppressed anger and drained by nervous exhaustion, he next devoted himself to the novel challenge of tying-up to a fixed dock. In his present emotional state, the task of judging how much free line was needed to allow for the lifting of the boat by the next flood (high tide) was confounding. At first Nicole offered to assist, but quickly stopped and stepped back—puzzled and hurt by his awful mood and flood of invectives. Finally, Lou finished tying-up, and blurted out, "I probably got it all wrong.

Nothing went right today." He kept the more negative thoughts to himself, *How in the world did I think this was going to be fun!*

Inevitably Lou cooled down. Likely the beer he dug out of their shopping bags helped. Somewhat composed and relaxed, with only a hint of irritation, he briefly told Nicole about the gear malfunction. She was stunned, and in a high-pitched agitated voice suggested, "You ought to sue the bastards. Your life was carelessly put at risk, and the boat potentially demolished." Lou sat quietly, nodded in agreement and sipped the beer. Somehow her vituperative tirade had an agreeable calming effect as it washed over him. He relaxed and was able to refocus away from frustration and start to think about repairing the gear problem.

The I/O's power switch that tipped the outdrive up out of the water, suddenly came to mind. This made servicing access easy, he had been told. It was another advantage of the I/O, particularly for changing the propeller. In contrast, a boat with an inboard engine and shaft connected to a traditionally fixed propeller, had to be hauled out of the water to change its propeller. *What do I have to lose,* he pondered. *I'll take a look inside the outdrive, before I seek help.* So he elevated the outdrive, and removed the metal cover—as he had observed back at the dealer's. The assorted drive levers and the propeller were in clear view. After a few minutes he turned to

Nicole, who was silently brooding in the cockpit, and asked for her help. He showed her the shift lever, and with the engine off, demonstrated how to move it into reverse, and then how it jammed when moved into forward. Lou then went to the stern to observe the outdrive, and told Nicole to move the gear into reverse. As she pulled the switch into reverse, the outdrive lever moved appropriately. Then he told her to try to move the gear into forward position. Her attempt to move into forward caused the outdrive lever to hit an obstacle. Clearly here was the problem. Lou concluded to himself, *no doubt that when the new propeller was installed, the young mechanic had likely removed this critical rod and replaced it backwards.* He then decided that it wouldn't require a master mechanic to correct the problem. With a few simple tools he disconnected the troublesome rod, turned it around, and reinstalled it facing the opposite direction. The gear shift now moved easily not only into reverse, but also smoothly into forward. Lou glowed with satisfaction and pride at his repair and Nicole clapped loudly.

A first of much to come, He thought, *maybe boating wasn't such a big mistake. I'm going to like tinkering with the boat as I learn more.*

Nicole couldn't help smile approvingly at his accomplishment; was particularly pleased at his dramatically improved mood; and she grabbed him in a hug with passionate abandon. The physical contact was what they needed after a stressful day. They relaxed, looked each other in the eye and spontaneously started laughing.

Finally, Nicole said, “Well, skipper, let’s hope we got the bugs out of this yacht of ours. When I drove in I spotted a couple of restaurants in town. We need to lighten-up and celebrate with a good dinner.”

CHAPTER THREE

The LowerYard (LY) was small by any standards, lacked basic facilities of any kind, and to call it a marina was an overly generous stretch. It was only a secure mooring for small recreational boats. At this early stage in Lou's boating experience, he was insensitive to the LY's limitations. His focus was on his new boat, and as far as he knew all marina's were the same. Without much thought, he likely assumed the old, weathered, deteriorated look was universal, and accepted it as part of the nautical charm. But, before long, after having seen other marinas, he learned that the LY's aged wooden docks were not the current standard, but were sadly behind the times and truly archaic.

An unwelcome finding at the LY was the numerous colonies of bold, large, black, carpenter ants who feasted on their favorite food (wood), and apparently were longtime residents. From the ant's viewpoint, the wooden docks provided an inexhaustible supply of delicious food.

Lou quickly connected all the empty ant spray cans he noticed in the dumpster with the scope of carpenter ant infestation. They boldly scampered all over the wooden docks. The LY was clearly in a state of general neglect and decay. Lou predicted, "With the help of the ants the LY's eventual collapse will surely occur sooner than later."

Routine use of ant spray effectively protected the boats from their assault. Though the fiberglass hulls were immune to ant attack, much of the interior wood trim, often of expensive teak, would be a choice treat for the ants. Therefore, the protocol depended on frequent spraying of the adjacent dock, along with the nylon mooring lines, which would afford the predatory and curious ants easy access to the boat.

Some of the newer marinas had gone so far as to install metal docks. Though resistant to the depredations of ants and the highly adverse effect of saltwater, they were costly and slippery when wet. Obviously, everything has its downside.

Besides looking old, the LY's fixed docks failed in a most fundamentally functional way: They were incapable of rising or falling with the tidal changes, since the docks were firmly bolted to the pilings. In waters that are subject to tidal changes—such as the Hudson River—the fixed docks create a burdensome as well as somewhat 'iffy' mooring process. First of all, with fixed docks, boats must never be tightly fastened to them, and sufficient slack must be left in the lines. The slack is essential to accommodate the rise and fall of tidal water—which in turn lifts or lowers (only) the boat, since fixed docks can't move. The amount of slack required isn't obvious, and is difficult for beginners to estimate. If there weren't enough slack, then extreme tension in the lines during tidal peaks risked serious boat damage, such as pulling the cleats out of the boat. The amount of slack depended on the range of tidal changes, which differ day-to-day in a given area, as it does along all tidal locations. Modern sailors have the good fortune to rely on the *Eldridge Tide and Pilot Book*, for precise tidal information. These useful tables accurately provide the time of the onset of flood and ebb, along with the maximum expected velocity of the water's flow.

Naturally, in early days, Lou was unaware of the existence of this invaluable resource, and struggled with moorings at the LY.

In response to the dramatic expansion of recreational boating, the commercial marina industry built floating docks throughout. In this nautical world, consumer preferences affected a positive change. Accordingly the floating docks, to which vessels can be firmly moored, rise and fall together with the changes in the tidal water level. Routine moorings were thus straightforward, fairly rapid, efficient, and tidal changes could be ignored..

From the onset Lou had learned about fenders, since they came with the boat and their use had been explained. The fenders are routinely lowered over the side of the boat towards the dock, and suspended by nylon lines. When docking, these heavy, long, tubular devices, usually made of rubber, are deployed to provide an invaluable protective interface between boat and dock.

For the most part, wooden hulls had become obsolete. Their vulnerability to rot, and need for frequent repainting and repair doomed them. The relatively light weight fiberglass constructed hulls, introduced in the 1960's, quickly replaced wood, particularly for recreational boats. With their outer coating of a polyester resin called 'gel-coat' that shielded the fiberglass from the damaging effects of the sun's rays, a lustrous brilliance to the hull was also created. Fiberglass has many virtues: never needs painting; won't rot; withstands indefinite immersion in water; and needs little or no maintenance—except for periodic removal of the pernicious marine barnacles from the bottom of the boat. Barnacles are tiny ubiquitous marine crustaceans that attach to the bottom of all boats, and form dense colonies. These irregular masses of barnacles cause a serious drag and roughness to boat movement. The resulting increase in fuel consumption caused by the drag of the barnacles is an important concern. Regular removal of the barnacle encrustations restores the smooth surface of the boat's bottom and its handling. It is advised to coat the freshly-cleaned bottom with an anti-fouling copper-containing paint to prevent recolonization of the barnacles. This paint has been in long use, but is only partially effective. The development of better antifouling materials and methods are on-going.

The critical weakness of fiberglass is its vulnerability to hull fracture if subjected to a forceful blow—such as an inadvertent collision with a dock, or another boat—if unprotected by fenders. When mooring lines of boats are firmly fastened to cleats on floating docks, with fenders in place, maximum safety and stability of the vessel is achieved, with minimal effort. Novice captains quickly master this technique.

Despite Lou's considerable relief in securing a slip for his boat, and his obvious excitement, the drawbacks of the LY were quickly adding up. He decided that he could live with the ant situation since it was at least manageable, though annoying. However, the entrance to the LY from the river presented an ongoing worrisome encounter. Every time he passed through this narrow gap. Lou's tension mounted, along with an attack of stomach cramps. He feared a collision with either a huge half-submerged barge on one side or an intimidating old wooden piling on the other. Helpfully, Lou was advised by his neighbors in the LY that the safest way to navigate through the passage was at fairly high speed, so as to resist the force of the river's current—running counter to the boat's direction—which threatened to dash the boat sideways against one or the other obstructions. Then, once through, speed must immediately be throttled back, almost to a full stop, to avoid running into nearby boats in the confined space of the LY.

Besides providing a home for Lou's boat, it turned out that the LY's choice location perhaps offset all its negatives. The Yard was right at the foot of the main street in the charming village of Nyack. Now Lou understood why the LY stayed filled to capacity and survived, despite its deplorable condition. A few steps from the boats were restaurants, food stores, assorted retail shops, and a number of antique shops. During the summer months, the town hosted occasional street fairs, which Lou and Nicole enjoyed. They soon selected as their favorite a small intimate restaurant that offered a consistently upscale French-cuisine. After a day's boating Lou and Nicole oftentimes enjoyed eating there, frequently with friends. With the convenience of the LY within walking distance, they could leisurely indulge in wines with the meal, without concern for the need to drive anyplace afterwards. If by chance Lou over-imbibed, as could happen, Nicole was there to steady him onto the boat to prevent his falling into the water.

***

Little by little Lou became familiar with the nautical world. It was like learning a foreign language. For instance, there was an important difference between a boatyard and a marina. During the recreational boating fervor of the 1960's and into the 1980's, new elegant marinas were built, and old ones upgraded. In a way the marinas were like private clubs—only open to all who could afford the tariff—replete with swimming pools, showers, laundry facilities, restaurants, and of course shops offering marine apparel and other luxury items. A weekend cruise to an attractive marina, often for extended stays became very popular, with reservations in advance being required to insure a slip during the sailing season. The marinas compete for the business of these boaters, who are by and large a financially-affluent urbanite group, with little or no boating experience. They own fine vessels, and want all possible creature comforts in a marina.

But, repair service facilities are rarely available at marinas. Most novice boat owners usually lack mechanical know-how of their own, and eventually recognize that their boats were vulnerable to frequent repair, of one sort or another. A mechanic expressed it well to Lou when he told him, "To imagine the strain on a boat engine, think of it as a car continuously going uphill in low gear. That's what it's like pushing a boat through the water. And in addition, the vessel is in corrosive saltwater which eats away at most everything, especially metal and can affect electronic equipment. It's surprising boats survive as well as they do."

The boatyards on the other hand, were the service facilities of the marine world, only they were few in number and located widely apart. If the boat engine failed, one can't get out and walk to the nearest gas station for help, as you could with a car. Therefore, prudence dictated a program of preventive maintenance at the highest possible level. Interested boat owners did well to learn some basics about engine problems, and a few simple troubleshooting measures. Such skills can prove invaluable to keep the boat going long enough to reach a boatyard.

If cost is an issue, best to reconsider powerboat ownership. Maybe a small sailboat would suffice.

***

A special breed of men inhabit boat-yards. They appear rough and not particularly welcoming, but possess expertise and arcane skills, which in many instances have been passed down generations. Paradoxically, though they are delighted with the increased income from the flood of pleasure boaters, their manner could be off-putting. It's often a communication impasse. Many of the new boat owners' urban/suburban orientation does not prepare them for the ethos of the marine world. Their ignorance about marine technology and maintenance can lead to frustrating interactions. Take the following dialogue about repair of a dented propeller, for example.

A twin engine boat ran over a floating log when thoughtlessly cruising on the river in the too-early spring. During that time of the year the river is filled with the jetsam and flotsam of the seasonal runoff, and the captain was too impatient to start his boating season. When the log hit, alarming vibrations could be felt throughout the boat, which typically signaled that at least one of the propellers had been struck. The captain cursed his luck and headed directly for the boatyard. Fortunately they weren't busy and one of the mechanics was available.

"O.K. let's get her lifted up and see what ya did," calmly said the mechanic.

The huge travel-lift moved out over the boat and soon lifted it far enough out of the water to gain visual access to the propellers. Sure enough a blade on the starboard prop was badly bent. The upset boat owner asked in a rather crisp, though restrained voice, "How long will it take you to bang it straight?"

They were both standing side by side on the dock looking up at the boat. The contrast in the two men was noteworthy. The boat owner was late middle-age, clean-shaven, of a stocky five-ft eight or nine inches in height, somewhat overweight, and dressed in a coordinated blue and white outfit with a captain's peaked-cap jauntily perched on his bald head. His dark brooding, squinting eyes peered out through sunglasses, and his pale face was distorted with concern and frustration as his jaws furiously worked on a large wad of chewing gum.

The tall, lanky mechanic, likely in his mid to late thirties, towered over him, with a many-days growth of whiskers covering his long, angular face. His manner seemed relaxed with hands tucked into the back pockets of his grease-stained bib-coveralls, and his blue eyes twinkled with good-humor. An old, soiled baseball cap was tipped back, with locks of overgrown blond hair over his forehead. He quietly absorbed the question, shook his head, and after a while answered, "Oh, we don't bang them out, as ya put it. It has to be sent out to a prop specialist." He hesitated, turned to look directly at the customer, and with a slight knowing smirk continued, "Along with the port prop."

"What!" was the owner's bark-like reply. He almost shouted as his voice pitched higher with exasperation. The compounding of costs and inconveniences was sinking in. He felt as though he was in water helplessly over his head."Why in the world do you have to send both?" finally was blurted out.

Luke, the mechanic, paused, pushed his cap back and scratched his head as though mulling over the strange question. He took a deep breath and explained slowly, as though talking to a child, "You see, Sir, . . . to straighten out the bend they must also grind and polish . . . which changes the weight some. Now with your twin screw . . . you want to properly balance the boat, don't ya? So both props must weigh exactly the same." He stopped to allow it all to sink in.

No one spoke for a while. Finally the owner, after absorbing this bit about propeller balancing, asked in a subdued voice, "How long does that take?"

"Oh, somewhere around a couple of weeks," answered Luke.

"Good lord, that means my boat will be laid-up here in the 'yard." Then he hastily added, "How about if I buy a couple of new props?"

"Sure can. Of course we have to special order 'em. Can't stock all the different sizes and configurations." Luke had been here before, and understood he now had the owner on a buyer's hook. So, he added with a big smile, "I'll make sure we get 'em in a couple of days, and have ya back in the water before ya know it."

With a sigh the resigned owner replied, "OK then. Please order them." He was emotionally drained by then, and hadn't even thought to ask about the cost. He knew the grand total for this fiasco would be considerable. He mentally reviewed what the repair involved: *hauling the boat out of the water, repairing the props, the cost of two new props, and he shouldn't forget the labor charges involved. Ugh!*

The following day it suddenly dawned on him, *why bother repairing the damaged ones when I'm buying new props?* Quickly he reached for the phone and called the Boatyard. To his dismay, he was told the damaged props had already been shipped for repair. As he hung up he mumbled to himself, *Could have predicted that's what they'd say. So I'll have spares. Just what I needed. They say extras of everything is important. Maybe I should even tow an extra boat along?* He nodded his head, and with a smile concluded, *I asked for it. Nobody made me buy a boat. But I'm learning what it's all about, and I think once I adjust it'll be fun . . . I hope.*

For many first time boat owners, especially the affluent, adjusting to their total dependence on boatyard personnel is a lesson in humility and reality. There simply are no opportunities for customary shopping around for best price. Either you serviced your own boat, or were grateful that the local yard did it for you.

What was called for was not difficult. Boat owners had to exercise patience when seeking help. At times, there might be a long wait for your turn with the mechanic. Of course, a fluency with the nautical lingo will help the interaction and speed the service. Always express gratitude for the service. When goodwill and good cheer were brought to the encounter, the people at the boatyard are delighted to assist and welcome the friendship.

CHAPTER FOUR

The measure of a skipper is not dependent on the size or elegance of his boat, but is earned by demonstrated boat-handling skill, especially with twin engine vessels. The beauty of the twin engine configuration is that it creates unlimited steering possibilities. Most notably, the difficulty backing to port with the single inboard engine is totally overcome. With twin engines the boat can literally be turned in a circle, pivoting at one spot.

This maneuverability is usually not called upon when cruising on the open water, but is essential when entering a marina where the boat's progress must be reduced to idle speed to avoid creating a wake that could damage the marina itself or boats moored there.

At idle speed, usually under five knots—approximately equivalent to five miles per hour—the rudders don't work and thus the boat can't be steered as usual with the helm (wheel).

In order for the rudders to function the boat's speed must allow for a flow of water to collide against the rudders with sufficient force. At speeds of five knots and lower the velocity of the water is inadequate. Steering then must be managed by using the engines—a not very easily mastered skill.

Each engine has two vertical levers, positioned on the control console at the steering station. These four levers are conveniently clustered close together. One lever is the accelerator: the further forward it's moved the faster the prop spins and so goes the boat. The other lever is the clutch with three positions: straight up is neutral; pushed forward moves the boat ahead; and pulled back moves the boat sternward. These back or forward boat movements are effected by appropriate rotation changes of the props: clockwise for forward and counterclockwise for backward. The decision to move the boat in a particular fashion, and at a controlled acceleration, requires simultaneous placement of each of the four levers in a precise position. It's instructive how the forward power of one engine is counter-balanced by the sternward thrust of the other. Therefore, along with the opposing engine forces, judicious acceleration changes of one or the other engine can effect a specific vessel movement. It sounds complicated . . . and indeed is. But, with time and determination it can be learned. After all, it's not nuclear physics. Just requires serious, focused memorization, and practiced repetition.

Understandably, beginners find this a difficult exercise. It's the most challenging skill new skippers of twin screw boats will confront.

Watching an experienced skipper move a twin engine vessel, running at idle speed, through a series of maneuvers in tight marina quarters and finally spin the boat gently backwards into its slip, is likened to a virtuoso musician's performance. The skipper's hand adjustments of the engine levers, and (for instance) the violinist's graceful bowing and fingerboard placements, are both rapid, unhesitatingly accurate, bewilderingly casual, and an inspirational joy to observe.

***

Lou's decision for his first real cruise was exciting. After some weeks of getting settled and comfortable with the Yard, and working on his boat handling skills with short turns up and down the river for a mile or so in either direction, his vision expanded: he wanted to sail around the Island of Manhattan, with his single engine I/O.

While getting to know the boat, he checked the anchor locker which opened on the deck close to the bow. He found the manually deployed anchor appropriately attached to a sturdy nylon line, and to confirm that the line was firmly connected to the boat he removed the anchor and all the line. Since there wasn't a spool or mechanism around which to coil the line for storage in the locker, Lou fatefully decided it was important to fabricate one. He found a rough piece of drift wood for this purpose. Pleased with how neat the coiled line looked wrapped around the wood, he placed it back into the locker with the anchor on top. It all fit snugly in the locker, and his attention was drawn elsewhere. He would later pay dearly for this harebrained idea.

***

With a marine chart of the entire New York City area including its surrounding waterways spread out on the cabin table, Lou planned the route for his inaugural cruise. It made him feel like a seasoned sailor and responsible skipper.

So, all charged-up, Lou walked out of the cabin with the chart in-hand, to where Nicole was sunning herself, and asked, "How would you like to take a quick trip around Manhattan Island?"

Nicole, who was a rather reluctant participant in the boating venture (to put it mildly), turned to Lou, recognized his barely contained eagerness, smiled warmly and answered, "Love, whatever you say. You must feel as though you got the boat handling under your belt, so why not! I've been impressed how smoothly you bring the boat into the Yard, and tie it up so neatly. Even some of the guys around here smile approvingly."

Lou's face lit up with delight. He was relieved by her ready agreement. *Maybe she's coming around,* he thought."Great," he rapidly said, as though afraid she would change her mind if he didn't jump-in. "Here, let me show you the course I've plotted on the chart." With a finger to trace the passage he explained, "We'll cruise down the Hudson to the northern tip of Manhattan Island; turn into the Harlem River which runs on the Island's east side; sail down to its southern end; and then turn north back up the Hudson to Nyack."

After a few moments' pause, concerned that she might be losing interest, he tried to sound convincing as he added, "This circumferential cruise will be real easy. We'll be within coastal waters with recognizable land features all around to enjoy and to guide us. Seeing the city from the boat will be a thrill."

Nicole smiled, forced a laugh and said, "Sounds reassuring. With land always in sight we can't possibly get lost. Eh, my Captain?"

Lou nodded and smiled with pleasure at her lighthearted response, and thought, *Looks like we might be getting off to a good start.*

While busy planning the trip, he overlooked checking the depth of the water along his route. Fortunately, the neglect didn't matter and was only academic. All of his routes were along major commercial and recreational waterways, where there was more water than he needed for his shallow (four inch) draft boat.

As Lou's initial excitement calmed down, and his nervousness diminished, his confidence built and he started to pay better attention to the information on the marine charts. Safe boating depended on these charts: they showed land formations and significant features; crucial water depths; locations of underwater obstacles, e.g., rock formations; and displayed the invaluable channel buoys.

The planned route down the Hudson River and around the northern tip of Manhattan drew Lou's initial attention. His study of the chart showed that this first turn was thru a narrow passage that had both an ominous name, and a troubling railroad bridge crossing the gap. The original settlers, the Netherland Dutch, called attention to the hazards of this opening by naming it, *Spuyten Duyvil* (Devil's spout), a reference to the strong and wild tidal currents. On top of that concern, Lou wondered when the railroad bridge opened for boat traffic? He decided to call the railroad office for information about scheduled openings. All his investigative time and effort would prove an unnecessary waste, though most informative.

When he finally connected with someone in the office and asked about the railroad bridge over *Spuyten Duyvil,* he was greeted with a loud guffaw, followed by the comment, "What are ya talking about, buddy? That bridge has been out of use for years, since they redirected the tracks down along the Harlem River in the Bronx, instead of along the Hudson. By the way, it's called a *Swing Bridge*—designed to swing 90 degrees horizontally on a central pivotal support. The bridge was left permanently locked open, creating two clear water passages. Stay to your right, like you would on the highway. The old Dutchmen were right about the tricky, unpredictable currents in the gap, so best not to dawdle but gun it fast when going thru. Every once in a while we get reports of some damn fool boater crashing into the support. Never does any harm to the bridge, but the boats are usually totaled. Good thing they over-built bridges in the old days."

Lou thanked the clerk, and thought, *What a fool I've been. I bet everyone in the Yard knows all about that swing railroad bridge. Why didn't I simply ask one of the guys. Live and learn.*

***

Racing past the open bridge and thru *Spuyten Duyvil* went smoothly with room to spare. Lou was overjoyed—and secretly relieved—with how well he navigated this chancy opening, and couldn't help shouting out, "Yes, sir. That's the way to do it. Just like a real skipper." He looked over at Nicole and knew immediately that her blasé attitude had evaporated.

She was animated with excitement, and her clear green eyes were wide open with wonder. Above the roar of the engine he heard her yell, "Wow! That was some thrill. It was reminiscent of a roller coaster ride I had as a kid. I was part terrified and part loving the awesome sensations."

As they cruised into the Harlem River proper Lou throttled back to a slow-to-moderate speed. Nicole's emotional high had dramatically improved her mood. Instead of passive participation she now wanted to be involved, and launched a question. "You know, I was taught that rivers, by definition, began in the highlands and flowed downhill to larger bodies of water, such as oceans. Why do they call the Harlem a river? I can see from the chart that it's only a watery channel connecting the Hudson River and the East River. The same actually holds for the East River. It's also a channel, connecting the Long Island Sound in the east to the Hudson River at the southern end of Manhattan, where all the waters blend into the expansive Upper New York Bay." She smiled widely at Lou, obviously pleased with her recollections and ability to decipher the chart.

Lou smiled back with considerable delight at her interest, and replied, "You've raised a good question. Let's see what I can recall. These so-called rivers are part of the Hudson estuary system, or tidal river system, where the tides meet the stream's current. Incidentally, in a large river such as the Hudson, the tidal impact only causes directional flow changes in (about) the surface six feet, while the deeper waters move uninterrupted outward to the ocean. Back to your question. Evidently both the Harlem and East rivers were exceptions to the definition.. As far as I can tell, way back folks likely started calling them rivers, and it simply stuck."

"Say, where did you learn all that stuff?" asked Nicole.

Lou laughed and said, "I've been 'googling' on my computer. You don't want me to sound like a raw novice, do you?"

"OK, skipper," said Nicole with a welcome alacrity. "Just don't get carried away, forget to steer, and run us aground." On impulse she moved over and kissed him on the cheek.

Lou turned and quickly pulled her to him with one arm, returned her kiss but on the lips, and hugged her tightly with a full body embrace.

"Save it for later. lover," said Nicole as she slowly pushed away, with obvious reluctance . “For now better keep both hands on the wheel.”

`”Yes ma’m. Back to business. Since you’re in charge of the chart, see if you can name the bridges we go under, and it’ll be interesting to keep count of how many there are.”

Nicole checked the chart and said, “The first bridge was way overhead as we raced through ‘old’ *Spuyten Duyvil.* It supports a major North/South highway called the Henry Hudson Parkway. Next, right after it, came the Broadway Bridge. Amazing how many highways lace through the city. Looking ahead on the chart I find more bridges than I ever imagined. I can see we’re just approaching another one. It connects upper Manhattan with the Bronx, and is called the University Heights Bridge. Its name likely was inspired by the large sprawling college campus in the adjacent Bronx, formerly known as New York University with its famous Hall of Fame for Great Americans—now called The Bronx Community College. You know, this chart has incredible information. We’re getting quite an education.”

Everything was going well including the weather, which for an early summer day couldn’t have been nicer. The cool refreshing breeze that fanned them in the open cockpit of the boat was a treat, and the sparkling blue sky—shaded to indigo in the west—filled with slow-moving, thin, random accumulations of gossamer-like white cumulus clouds, created a stunning canopy. Lou and Nicole exchanged knowing looks, as the boat slid smoothly through the calm river waters. All tensions faded as they were caught up in the enjoyable novel boating experience.

They were surprised at how few people were spotted, though the city was humming with heavy auto traffic ceaselessly moving on both sides of the river. Nicole whimsically commented, “This huge city looks odd with its millions hidden away somewhere. They certainly couldn’t be crammed into the automobiles that I see all over the place. Interesting how the continuous flow of cars kind of reminds me of a colony of ants, where the queen is safely guarded in her underground kingdom and, like the cars, the streams of worker ants are outside foraging for food.”

“A creative analogy, Nicole. Only these modern scavengers are all hustling for themselves. Except in rare instances, none have any sense of collective or community obligation, as in the ant world. On the other hand, it’s likely some few folks might happen to take notice of us cruising along, adorned in our short pants, boating sneakers, dark sun glasses, peaked captain’s hats, and assume, incorrectly I might add, that we’re a couple of very rich pooh-bahs. Along with envy; some might even resent us.”

“Right-oh, skipper. Now head's up for some major bridges. Say, look at this. Wonder of wonders. I see real people walking across a bridge. Let’s hope none are disgruntled citizens, who might decide to anoint us with rotten garbage as we pass under. The first bridge is the older Washington Bridge, which appears like it has been there a long time, with huge masonry supports at either end of the span. Right alongside is a somewhat larger, obviously more modern span, called the Alexander Hamilton Bridge. It’s a major link in a vast network of roads.

"Just listen to this. A mind boggling complex of major roads feeds in all directions, beginning with the George Washington Bridge which spans the Hudson River from New Jersey. Drivers coming into Manhattan can go directly onto an express road to the Alexander Hamilton Bridge and cross the Harlem River into the Bronx to connect with a choice of highways. The chart’s depiction of the many complex clover-leaf exits at all junctions, makes me nervous. If I were driving there I would probably get hysterical, take the wrong ramp, and end up completely lost.” They both laughed, since she was a notoriously timid driver, and her comment held more truth than hyperbole.

“Nicole, the next bridge up ahead is different. I happened to have read about it. It’s called the High Bridge, and was constructed as an aqueduct to bring water to Manhattan from reservoirs upstate. The original design incorporated a series of stone arches, which look very much like those built by the ancient Romans for their aqueducts. Some of those old Roman aqueducts are still standing, so why not copy them. The bridge never carried vehicles and was strictly for pedestrian use. As you can see, the main span over the river now has a modern steel arch, which replaced the numerous old river-crossing arches. I imagine the narrow openings of the arches restricted boat use on the river. Fortunately, a number of these classical stone arches were retained on the Bronx side. Currently it's closed to the public during restoration. I understand that the original High Bridge aqueduct is no longer in service, and has been replaced by massive tunnels that bring the precious water into the city. As an additional note of interest, the High Bridge was the first bridge built in the city."

"You know, Lou, I never gave any thought to where water came from. Like most people, I turn the faucet and expect the water, hot or cold, to reliably appear. Shows you how spoiled we are to take something so essential as water for granted. Well. the High Bridge makes it six bridges so far, and there are many more to come."

Nicole, highly amazed at the number of additional of bridges that crossed the River, enjoyed calling out their names as they lined up in fairly close order: the Macombs Dam; the 145th Street; the Madison Ave.; the Park Ave.; the 3rd Ave.; the Willis Ave.; and the Triboro, which she explained, "The Triboro Bridge was a major connecting highway from Manhattan, across Randall's Island, on through Queens with links to both La Guardia and Kennedy Airports."

As they approached the junction, where the watery channel (problematically named a river) of the Harlem River ended and become known as (also problematically named) the East River, they passed under a pedestrian bridge which connected Manhattan with Randall's Island, called Wards Island Foot Bridge. "If I counted right," reported Nicole, "that's 14 bridges so far."

CHAPTER FIVE

"Nicole, we're now entering a special place on the Harlem River, at a point almost exactly midway down Manhattan's east side. As you can see, the passage widens considerably. I'm going to slow the boat so we can take it all in. When we pass Randall's Island, look to your left, or port, and you'll see the East River flowing in from the Long Island Sound. That section of the East River, extending back towards the Sound for about one mile, is called Hell Gate—the most unruly stretch of water on this entire complex of passages. Wow, just look at that violent water. Hell Gate's worse than I expected. Those vicious looking waves are rolling in all directions, and over on the far side I even see a huge whirlpool spinning rapidly."

"Looks scary to me," said Nicole. "Glad we're not going through there. Any idea why it's like that? It's as though there's an invisible line in the water separating Hell Gate from the nice calm waters of the Harlem."

"Yes, quite a sight. I'll fill you in later on Hell Gate's dynamics and history. Now I'm going to turn to port so as to avoid that little island on our right sitting in the middle of the

River, called Mill Rock Park. We have to pass closer to Hell Gate, but don't worry. We'll cruise past and head down to the southern end of Manhattan as planned, on what is now called the East River."

As the boat swung in a slow curve near the edge of the turbulent waters of Hell Gate, without any warning signs, the worst possible happened—the engine died.

Lou was stunned, and for a moment was paralyzed with disbelief. Visions of an impending calamity flashed into his mind—loss of control of the boat at this hazardous junction was serious and frightful. He realized that unless he could get the motor started they were in real danger. In desperation he elected to force the motor into action by pushing the throttle all the way forward to give it a heavy jolt of gas—an unwise decision. It failed to work, and likely only succeeded in flooding the engine. Frantically he tried repeatedly to start the engine. He did everything he could think of, but the motor wouldn't turn over.

As fear mounted, a cold sweat broke out on his forehead, his gut went into wrenching spasm, and the vessel started to inescapably slip into Hell Gate. With a sense of failure, he finally gave up trying to start the engine. He couldn't avoid the looming danger.

Lou gasped for breath and felt his heart racing. An unsettling mix of emotions caused him to feel dizzy and nauseous—his fear had provoked an attack of vertigo. Besides the frustration and anger at the engine's failure, he experienced near-debilitating panic and helplessness. Overwhelmed with despair, he frantically reached for the marine radio, and shouted "May Day, May Day." ('*someone please help me*' was what he meant).

Lou instantly knew that the call for help was a futile wasted effort, and felt abashed at his senseless hysterical act. It was obvious that even if the Coast Guard heard his appeal, there was no way they, or any other boat for that matter, could reach them in time to help.

In addition to Hell Gate's tremulous waters which bounced the powerless boat precariously, he noted with alarm that they were drifting to the left, where just barely covered with water he spied a massive rock outcropping.

The horrible reality shocked and flustered Lou, but paradoxically the crisis also energized his focus with increased clarity. Over and above his emotional turmoil—feeling like a drowning man with his head struggling to stay above the water (a sickening déjà vu recall)—he tenaciously clung to the belief that survival and avoidance of disaster were possible. It was up to him, and him alone. *But what to do?*

Painfully he struggled with doubt and uncertainty as the boat continued to flounder. Suddenly, like an electrical shock, he had a startling thought: he knew what had to be done. An obvious solution to the crisis was at hand, and Lou shouted, "Of course . . . how stupid can I be . . . Why didn't I think of it sooner . . . I must immediately drop the anchor to stop our drifting."

Before he climbed out of the cockpit, he turned to Nicole who looked terribly frightened: she fiercely clutched herself with crossed arms; her face had a look of terror as she stared fixedly at the water; and, though speechless at the moment, her open mouth was poised to scream. Lou shouted to get her attention, and rapidly explained what he was going to do.

"Nicole, I'm going out to drop the anchor. And you must try to start the engine." Lou's commanding voice cut through her incapacitating fear, and she awkwardly, as though just awakening from a stupor, stumbled to the controls. But their operation was beyond her. She thought, *that was Lou's job, I never paid any attention to what he was doing*. Avoiding his eyes, she stammered with a trembling voice, "Lou, I don't know how to do it." "It's easy," he yelled, and hastily showed her the simple procedure.

There was no time to review the directions and confirm whether she understood. The critical priority was to lower the anchor. Without so much as a backward glance at Nicole, he lunged forward on the heaving deck, holding firmly onto the railing with one hand for security, intent on quickly reaching the anchor locker in the bow.

Releasing the anchor into the water sparked a sudden awareness that he was not only ignorant of the water's depth at this point in Hell Gate—so didn't know how much anchor line to let out—but also, even more basically, he didn't know the length of his anchor line. Nonetheless, the anchor offered the only hope of controlling the boat, so he rapidly worked to get it out.

On top of all this, Lou was chagrined to discover that the old scrap of wood (around which he had amateurishly wrapped the line) critically impeded the anchor line's necessary rapid release. As he fumbled to spin the wood to unravel the line, furious with his own stupidity, he deeply cut a finger on a sharp edge of the wood. The dripping blood soon decorated the white deck with bright red globs, which Lou ignored while he struggled at his task. In addition, maintaining balance on the heaving deck was difficult, and he had to frequently grab the railing for safety.

With all the anchor line out, it didn't take long for him to sadly conclude that the boat's drift hadn't slowed. He subsequently learned that the depth at this location far exceeded his length of anchor line. Therefore, the anchor never reached bottom where it could dig in for a hold.

Just at that critical moment, when all seemed lost, to his astonishment, relief, and incredible joy he heard and felt the engine roar into life.

***

When Nicole spotted the blood dripping from Lou's hand, she released the throttle, which was at full power, and shrieked in horror, "My God, what happened to you? You're bleeding all over the boat. It must be a terrible injury." Lou jumped down into the cockpit and mumbled, "It's nothing, don't worry about it. What's important is that you started the engine." He leaned over, kissed her on the cheek, eased the throttle, forced a smile, and added, "What do ya know! All that stubborn engine needed was a woman's touch."

Cautiously he slowly backed the boat out of Hell Gate. Though his heart was still pumping rapidly, his troubled mind had settled and cleared. He knew that if he turned the boat bow first, there was a good chance he would run over the anchor line—still hanging in the water—and either cut it, or even worse, tangle it in the prop, possibly bend a blade, and stall the engine again. So, he deliberately backed the boat out of Hell Gate, with the anchor safely dragging off the bow. After entering well into the calm waters of the Harlem River he cautiously pointed the bow north—back up the Harlem—slowed the motor to idle speed, and turned the wheel over to Nicole with the instructions,

"Nicole, this will be easy for an old seaman, or is it seawoman, like you. Please take the wheel, stay in the middle of the Harlem, and don't touch the throttle. I'm going out to the bow to haul up the anchor. It'll take only a few minutes." Trying hard to sound calm and confident to help reassure Nicole, who still looked wan and tense, he called out as he hastened to the bow, "Everything's under control, love. Sorry, but the excitements all over. We'll skip the trip we planned to go around Manhattan, and do it another day. Steer the good ship back the way we came, and off to home we go."

***

They cruised along silently with Lou at the helm, as they both recovered, and tried to calm down from the trauma and fright of Hell Gate. Finally, unable to restrain herself, Nicole poured out her feelings in an emotional outburst. "Lou, I've never been so scared in my life. I was sure the boat would sink and we'd drown. I can't get that fearsome whirlpool out of my mind. I had visions of the boat being pulled into it, quickly sucked under, and we horribly die. I'm going to have nightmares about that for some time. Tell me, why in the world are the waters in Hell Gate so dangerous?"

When she paused to catch her breath, Lou said, "Before I get into that, tell me how you started the motor."

"Actually, I was so terrified and upset at the time, that I don't remember anything. I seem to have blocked out the entire episode. I imagine I did what you told me, but how, what, and when, is a blank. If you asked me right now how to start the motor, I couldn't tell you. The only thing I remember is seeing the blood dripping from your hand, and thinking you had a terrible accident. Maybe somehow you cut off a finger. At that moment I felt woozy and almost fainted. Everything was going unbelievably wrong. One horrible thing happened after another. By the way, how's the finger doing? Looks like that large band aid is working well to control the awful bleeding. Good thing you thought to bring along a first aid kit." She turned to look at him with a broad smile, and added, "Thanks of course to your indoctrination as a Boy Scout that you remembered the old motto, 'be prepared.'"

With Nicole back at the controls, safely keeping the slow moving boat in mid-channel, and the River momentarily devoid of other traffic, Lou decided it was a good time to clean up the blood stains before they dried. With a supply of paper towels and a handy Windex spray bottle, it didn't take long to remove all traces of the blood.

Nicole seemed to have relaxed as she sat next to Lou, who had resumed control of the helm. Lou reached across and gently squeezed her hand and asked, "Are you ready to learn about Hell Gate's troubled waters?"

After a deep sigh, she answered, "I'd appreciate a sound, reasonable, explanation. That place terrorized me. It seemed bewitched and filled with malevolent spirits, so cold facts are welcome to help dispel my imagined horrors."

"I'll try, love. It's somewhat complicated, so stop me if I'm not coming across. It helps if you look at the chart as I go on . . . Basically, the confluence of unique geographic features doubtlessly are the main factor in creating the difficult waters of Hell Gate. A collision occurs at Hell Gate when the Hudson River's downstream force meets the unimaginable power of the Atlantic Ocean's tidal impact.

"In a flood tide, when the ocean surges into the Hudson River, the flow comes in from two directions—on one hand, the Atlantic Ocean pushes through the Long Island Sound and enters Hell Gate's constrictions; and at the same time the Ocean also enters New York harbor and drives up the East River to Hell Gate. The flood tide also pushes up the Hudson and causes the Harlem to flow down to Hell Gate. To make the situation worse, the narrow confines of Hell Gate have been rigidly defined with the construction of sturdy concrete and stone walls on either side to prevent the otherwise inevitable erosion of the vulnerable embankments. Therefore, as the waters mix at Hell Gate with cataclysmic turmoil, they bounce off the confining walls, ricochet back and forth, and create water agitation in random crosscurrent directions, some of which evolve into the formation of a whirlpool. At times the currents in Hell Gate have been known to reach velocities of 5.0 knots, or more. A considerable force for skippers to take into account. In addition, the active waters of Hell Gate are significantly disrupted when vessels increase acceleration to overcome Hell Gate's turbulence, and create their own powerful wake action (commercial ships, e.g., tugboats, which often travel these waters, leave colossal wakes). All these forces—collision of tidal flows, confining walls, and wake activity—combine to increase the incredibly haphazardous and chaotic movements of the water. For small boats, the safest time to plan passage through Hell Gate is during slack water. This is an hour-long interval, during which ebb and flood tides have abated, and the water is calm."

"Good lord," responded Nicole. "What a mess. Can't they do something?"

"Historically, Hell Gates' problems were recognized back in colonial times," continued Lou. "But due to its critical value as a connecting passage, much commerce has always challenged the dangers. Many an intrepid skipper who felt he could manage the angry waters, nevertheless, floundered on the huge rocky reefs that existed in the middle of Hell Gate—a major navigational obstacle. It wasn't until the late 1880's that the U.S. Army Corps of Engineers succeeded in blowing up enough of the rocks to eliminate the menace."

CHAPTER SIX

For many recreational boat owners the lure of moving-up to a bigger, more powerful boat borders on the irresistible. Such was the case with Lou. He offered as justification that two engines were safer, and said, "After all, there's little chance of both engines failing at the same time." Then for emphasis in an unequivocal tone of finality he added, "I never again want to depend on a boat with only one engine."

So, at the beginning of the second boating season, Lou didn't take long to settle on a twin-screw cabin cruiser for his next boat. His eyeballs almost rotated when he talked about it. From the time he found a dealer with the boat he wanted and settled financial arrangements, he couldn't wait to take possession.

Nicole compliantly nodded in silent agreement, with her memories of Hell Gate still fresh. But, if she were honest, and asked for an opinion (which she wasn't), there was no doubt that her predictable answer would be, '*Sell the damn boat as quickly as possible, and let's take up something like golf, or maybe tennis instead.*'

Moreover, Lou was off on a sort of manic quest for the boat of his dreams. His constant state of high-pitched animation affected all facets of his behavior, including an intensified sexual response to Nicole—which, incidentally, she quite enthusiastically welcomed. She had no illusions that somehow she could convince Lou to give up boating, so rationalized to herself, *Since we're committed to boating, a bigger twin engine boat made sense. Besides, this was a battle I know I couldn't win. But of course, as it turned out . . . I must admit that Lou's ongoing passionate mood is truly a delightful treat. I probably should think of it as a sort of well-earned compensation.*

The day Lou finally took possession of the new boat was hectic. He learned from prior experience to first obtain a slip before he signed for the new boat. He was lucky to get the last open slip at the Tarrytown Boat Club, where slips were limited in number, expressly for larger boats. It was a classic marina, directly across the Hudson River from Nyack on the north side of the Tappan Zee bridge, which featured a large club house with a surprisingly good restaurant, as well as a convenient gas dock.

Eager and impatient to pick up the new boat, Lou restlessly paced up and down with one eye on the clock, while at the same time concealing a measure of anxiety. Despite an outward appearance of confidence and macho assurance, Lou privately worried, *Am I going to be able to handle this new twin engine boat by myself? Coming down the river shouldn't be hard, but slowing to idle speed as I enter the marina, and then backing into the slip between another boat and the finger dock, will be a hell of a challenge.*

When the time came, he sailed his old boat (traded for the new one) a few miles upstream to the dealer's boatyard for the exchange, while Nicole remained in the Boat Club at their slip to assist in docking. It didn't take her long to become restless and anxious as time dragged. Though she was confident Lou could manage, she also knew he was nervous, and until the boat was safely in the marina she couldn't help worrying.

***

After accepting no more than thirty minutes of instruction (bare minimum) in the basics of twin engine operation—how to stop and go, make turns, and go forward and backward—Lou boldly took charge and headed out onto the Hudson River. Paradoxically, on one hand he barely could contain his exuberance, while on the other hand his undercurrent of angst mollified his joy. Fortunately, his worries about the weather and their vagaries which could create difficult boating conditions, faded with the day's unthreatening prospects. The cloudless bright blue sky and the favorable lack of wind combined to allow for pleasant sailing and easier docking. He smiled to himself at a passing thought, *Why, with my wrap-around sunglasses and captain's peaked hat I look like an experienced skipper, and maybe will fool folks. Now if I can only fool myself.*

Before long Lou started to feel uneasy. The boat's size, as compared to the old one, suddenly felt massive, and potentially almost unmanageable. His sense of confidence waned and he questioned his ability to safely bring her into the Club. Despite a growing darkened mood, along with an acute awareness of being perilously alone, he struggled to dismiss the negativity. Lou firmly grasped the helm up on the flying bridge with both hands in an angry gesture, straightened his posture, and mumbled to himself, *For better or worse, it's up to me. I know I can do it. A real piece of cake,* which he ardently repeated out loud.

After an uneventful trip of about 30 minutes, Lou warily approached the narrowed entrance to the Tarrytown Boat Club. He swallowed hard to void the bitter stomach reflux—an unwelcome response to his tension—and focused intently on the task at hand, while on an inner emotional level he braced for an impending calamity.

Intentionally Lou had selected a mid-week day to pick up the boat. He hoped not only for little traffic on the River, but also counted on only a few members, if any, to be around the Club to witness his arrival. On this inaugural voyage, he feared that the usual weekend crowds would likely tend to make him self-conscious and increase his already heightened nervousness.

To his surprise and incredulity, despite his tension and fear, he flawlessly succeeded in docking the boat on the first try. Lou couldn't help but to consider it a miracle, and intuitively attributed it to beginner's luck. *Next time*, he expected, *would be the real test*. Nicole greeted him with a broad smile and called out, "Well done, skipper," as she eagerly grabbed the mooring lines tossed to her, and efficiently tied them around the cleats. Lou shut down the engines, sighed to himself with considerable relief that somehow he managed docking without mishap, and climbed onto the dock. Nicole embraced him warmly. For a while in the otherwise quiet and empty marina, bathed in the comfort of a warm sun, they stood there all aglow with arms around each other, admiring their elegant cruiser. It was an auspicious beginning which drew them together in mutual delight. This rare moment was vaguely evocative of untold possibilities and promise.

Finally, while pacing up and down the finger dock to which the boat was tied, Lou could contain himself no longer and started to expound to Nicole, who was seeing the boat for the first time. "Isn't she a beauty," he said with obvious pride, sounding more like a statement of fact than a question. Unable to resist sliding his hand on the shiny, white hull, he continued, "Now let me tell you all about her."

Nicole learned more than she needed or wanted to know, but caught up in the moment's high-pitched drama she enjoyed listening to Lou's impassioned monologue.

"We'll have more power than you can imagine," Lou said. "Each of our two Crusader V-8 gas-fueled engines is rated at 270 horsepower. One alone could drive the vessel if need be. Don't forget to remind me to show them to you. If you can admire inanimate objects, then you'll certainly recognize that these blue-colored engines are beautiful. And most reassuring, Crusader engines have been around for over 50 years, with a well-earned record of dependability. They're made by GM, who based the marine models on Chevy's sturdy workhorse blocks."

When he paused to catch his breath, Nicole, trying to sound interested, chimed in with, "Lou, where did you learn all this great stuff?"

Looking pleased with himself, and coupled with a knowing nod, he replied, "It's important for a skipper to know all the specs of his vessel. I've still a lot to learn, but I made a good start while shopping around, reading all the literature, and asking lots of questions."

Lou bubbled so with pride that he almost stammered as he rambled on. “If anyone inquires, you should nonchalantly tell them that our boat has an overall hull length of 34 feet—to which is added almost two feet of pulpit bow extension, with the power-activated anchor attached beneath—and the boat’s width, or beam, is 12 feet 6 inches. Each engine is fed by its own 125 gallon gas tank, and I have the capability of redirecting the fuel to either engine, as circumstances might require. Naturally, since the tanks are mounted on opposite sides of the boat, it’s wise to drain them at the same rate to insure proper boat balance, whenever possible. In addition, we have a 40 gallon fresh water tank and a 12 gallon one for hot water. Therefore, just like at home, we can enjoy hot showers. And of course, for the preservation of the engines, they have built-in closed cooling systems filled with antifreeze solution. In contrast, when sea water is used to flush through the engines for cooling the corrosive impact prematurely destroys them.”

***

It was another one of those rare uplifting fair weather days. The morning’s azure blue sky was adorned with a scattering of slow moving white cumulus clouds which feebly blocked the solar rays. The brisk morning temperature would soon moderate as the sun warmed up, forecasting a delightful day of cruising on the River. Lou always enjoyed the early morning quiet. Few people were about, and he would sit up on the flying bridge with its commanding view of the marina and take in the sights for miles in all directions.

The air here in the marina—some 35 miles upstream from the Lower New York Bay— was different than inland. On the River, one knew the ocean wasn't far away. The air contained a touch of salinity, along with a trace of an aquatic fishy bouquet, born upstream on the Atlantic's cyclical flood and ebb. It was an environment a world apart which Lou relished. With his new boat and upscale marina, Lou was fulfilled and felt amazingly relaxed.

Lou and Nicole had invited friends to join them for a boat ride. Jane and Oscar arrived midmorning as expected, eagerly looking forward to the planned circum-navigation of the Manhattan Island—the same aborted trip Lou attempted in their old boat only to get involved in a frightening encounter with Hell Gate.

This wouldn't be Lou and Nicole's first circumnavigation. Several weeks ago they had made a trial run. Lou had insisted that the first long trip with the new boat should be around Manhattan. In other words, he felt they should complete the trip they hadn't finished. More than anything else, he wanted to demonstrate to Nicole that the hazards of Hell Gate could be readily avoided, and thus help overcome her fears. All went well on the trial cruise, and Nicole's anxieties were appreciably attenuated. No doubt, the larger, more powerful boat gave her an increased sense of security, and she was comforted by Lou's insistence that the new boat could now easily sail right through Hell Gate, if they so decided, without any trouble. "Besides," Lou retorted, "in order to get out into Long Island Sound for our planned cruises to many interesting ports and places, we must go through Hell Gate. I'll try to schedule the trip when it's slack water. But, just keep in mind that with our engines' combined total of 540 horsepower pushing us along, we'll go through Hell Gate—even at its worst—like a hot knife through butter."

Before Jane and Oscar arrived, Lou advised Nicole, "Best not to tell them about our misadventure with Hell Gate until we are well beyond it and reach the Hudson River at the southern tip of Manhattan. We don't want to unnecessarily alarm them. O.K.?"

"Sure thing, dear. Certainly makes sense," replied Nicole. "Besides, It'll take me a while to calm down inside after just looking at that fiendish Hell Gate place."

Anticipating a roundtrip of well over four hours, Nicole had prepared sandwiches, a large thermos of coffee, a container of ice tea, and brought along a generous supply of her favorite chocolate chip cookies. The flying bridge's comfortable seating for four would allow Nicole to serve lunch up there while the boat was underway.

Lou agreed, and added, "Good plan. With the favorable weather and the flat, tranquil water, we won't have trouble holding our dishes and cups steady. Jane and Oscar should truly enjoy themselves, sitting out in the fresh air, taking in the sights, listening to your travelogue about the bridges and, of course, eventually recounting our harrowing Hell Gate experience."

***

Jane's outgoing friendly personality drew a lot of attention, and was in sharp contrast to her husband. Though of a friendly nature, Oscar came across as withdrawn and indifferent. His slightly rounded shoulders and tipped-forward head were attributed by friends to his profession as an accountant where he spent long hours seated looking at financial documents.

In a social setting he seldom initiated conversation, and characteristically often hid behind his ever-present pipe—fussing with relighting it, or assiduously cleaning the bowl and stem. People wondered how Jane and Oscar got together. Yet, their marital success appeared obvious. The popular theory goes that their divergent personality quirks worked to offset each other. Oscar was happy to have Jane cover for his shyness, while he offered her calm stability and let her shine.

Men couldn't help being drawn to Jane. Her effortless enthusiasm was infectious. She seemed unaware of how physically attractive she was, and greeted all with a warm welcoming manner and easy smile. Lou wondered whether Nicole noted how he often got involved in lengthy conversations with Jane at social events. Furthermore, Jane was a good listener, and her questions and comments indicated a true interest and engagement, not a perfunctorily polite reply. Lou also admitted to himself that when in her company he couldn't help experience a pleasurable sexual arousal. So when Nicole suggested that they invite Jane and Oscar for a day of boating, Lou restrained his delight and appeared calm.

Lou was pleased at how Nicole graciously took charge of making their guests comfortable, and was surprised when she immediately began talking about the general marine environment. She sounded as if she were an 'old salt,' and had been around boating for years. Nicole also reviewed the main features of the boat, with emphasis on the two powerful engines—while slyly winking at Lou. Finally, with a knowing smile, she directed their attention to the head (toilet), and with a broadening grin added, "Just like at home, you should kindly flush when finished. Don't worry about fouling the water, since we have a holding tank for the waste, which is periodically unloaded into an approved receptacle." Everyone laughed as they settled in for a fun day.

Jane's delight with the boat was obvious from the moment she stepped aboard. She was too excited to sit, so stood next to Lou at the helm on the flying bridge with its wide commanding view, and watched his every move as the boat was slowly maneuvered out of the marina and into the Hudson River. In slow motion the boat gracefully turned to port, assumed a southerly course downstream, and passed under the Tappan Zee bridge. Nicole and Oscar paid no attention to the commencement of the trip, and they were contentedly engaged in conversation.

Nicole's manner about boating came across as knowingly nonchalant, and Oscar was satisfied to be seated smoking his pipe listening for the most part to Nicole.

Without a word of advance warning, Lou gradually increased the speed. In sync with the mounting acceleration, the boat's posture started to change: the bow began to rise progressively; and an increasingly turbulent track of waves were left aft. Jane hung on to the front rail and shouted, "Wow, Lou. It feels like you've turned us into a speedboat crashing through the water, tipped up on its rear end."

"Hang on, Jane," Lou called out "Right now we're forcing our way as we displace the water. If there was even a minor chop, we would feel the bounce. In a few moments something special will happen and all this will change."

Suddenly the bow dropped, and it felt as though the boat lifted up. It was dramatic. They were now skimming along on top of the water; the stern wake calmed down; and their speed increased. Jane turned to Lou with an amazed expression and asked, "My god, what did you do? I was watching carefully, and you didn't move your hands, nor change the throttles."

"I knew you would get a kick out of this. It's called planing," explained Lou. "Vessels with specially designed hulls automatically plane when they reach certain speeds. It's my impression that this boat is at the upper size limits where planing is possible. Notice how smoothly we are moving through the water. I will now slow the engines a bit and still be able to maintain the planing. Planing is not only fuel efficient, but also gives a more comfortable ride. Don't get the wrong idea about my grasp of much technical stuff. I'm a pragmatic skipper. As long as I know how to run the ship, I'm satisfied. Before we leave the subject, though, let me impress you with a bit I sort of memorized. 'When planing the boat's weight is predominantly supported by hydrodynamic lift'—whatever that is— 'rather than buoyancy when displacing the water'—which sounds like something to do with floating." He then laughed, adding, "So are you impressed?"

Jane marveled at how he handled the boat, and answered quickly with a feigned coquettish leer, "Lou, you're the best skipper I know . . . But to be honest, you're the only one." They laughed enjoyably together, as their relationship grew increasingly relaxed.

Lou turned to her and asked, "Would you like to hold the helm?"

Her eyes opened wide with surprise and said, "Can I? I would be thrilled. But don't leave me alone. It would be terrifying." Lou laughed and assured her he wouldn't budge. As they approached Spuyten Duyvil, Lou took over and slowed the boat. He turned towards the opening into the Harlem River; cautiously checked that the passage was clear and that no boat was approaching from the other direction; then powered up and raced through at high speed.

The dramatic rush between the huge stone railroad piers thrilled Jane and she spontaneously whooped and yelled with uninhibited delight, like a youngster on a roller coaster ride at the amusement park. Jane's loud shouts were infectious and drew Nicole and Oscar from their conversation into the momentary gaiety.

CHAPTER SEVEN

"Good lord," said Jane as they slowly sailed down the Harlem River. "How many bridges are there? I've lived in and around the City all my life and never realized there were so many bridges connecting Manhattan to the boroughs. Certainly unobservant of me."

"Counting down from Spuyten Duyvil to Hell Gate, which we'll talk about later," answered Nicole, "there are an incredible number of 14 bridges. Incidentally, the Harlem River lost its name at the junction with Hell Gate, and became simply known as the East River, which continues to flow down on the east side of Manhattan to the southern tip where it merges with the Hudson River."

"Well, Nicole," said Jane while shaking her head in a gesture of admiration, "you certainly are knowledgeable. I guess you and Lou have sailed these waters for years and enjoyed learning all the interesting things."

"Ha! You couldn't be further from the truth, my dear," declared Nicole. "This is actually only our second season of boating on the Hudson, and we're just getting to know it. And, since I'm too timid to take turns at the helm, by default I've become the untitled assistant navigator. That is, I read the chart and call out local features." Then looking at Lou with head tipped, she said in a casual manner, "After all, Lou's the skipper, which makes him chief honcho. I'm the lowly crew who takes care of everything else: which means my main job is to leap from the boat onto the dock with the mooring lines and tie-up securely. Depending on how close he backs the boat into the slip, at times the gap appears huge, and threatens life and limb for me to jump across." Then with a burst of laughter, she added, "It's an unglamorous job that doesn't pay much, but in compensation I do get to sleep with the lord and master."

Everyone, including Oscar, laughed. Lou turned from the helm and with a wide smile added, "Ain't she the lucky one," which provoked a second round of good cheer. The friendly banter helped create a lighter mood.

Though Jane laughed along with everyone else, she thought, *If I'm not mistaken, I detect an element of strain between the two of them. Could it be that Nicole isn't particularly happy with the boating? If I were in her place I'd be thrilled.*

Soon after passing Hell Gate, dead ahead right in the middle of the East River the long slender Roosevelt Island appeared, and surprised both Jane and Oscar who were only vaguely aware of its existence. Jane's interest was visibly aroused as she asked, "I see tall apartment buildings, so obviously people live there. How do they get back and forth from the Island? I heard about an aerial lift, but is that all?"

"Residents now-a-days have a choice," replied Nicole as she referred to a small notebook. "The first connection was built from Queens in 1955, and unimaginatively named the Roosevelt Island bridge. The aerial, called the Tramway, began operation in 1976, and a subway link to Manhattan was opened in 1989." Before anyone could respond she added with a pleasant smile, "This island and the bridges coming up are special. To be able to tell you about them without sounding like an idiot, I did some research and took notes. So we're really learning about them together. I hope you're interested?"

"Great job, Nicole. To be certain, we're interested," exclaimed Jane enthusiastically. "Thanks for taking the trouble. Please carry on."

Nicole smiled appreciatively at Jane, and resumed her talk. "The four bridges coming up are the last on the East River and arguably the most impressive crossings. As you will see, they span the widest stretch of the River and provide vital communication links that tie the City together. The first is the Queensboro Bridge, which we are soon to sail under. Its span passes over Roosevelt Island, and opened in March, 1909. Look up and you'll see the Tramway right next to and just before the bridge. I understand originally this bridge provided sole access to Roosevelt Island, but the connection was shut down years ago. As the name implies it connects the Borough of Queens to Manhattan. The three remaining bridges are up ahead, positioned fairly close together. I also found out that there are two tunnels under this stretch of the River, both of which connect to Queens: one is called the Queens Midtown Tunnel (for motor vehicles); and the other is the Pennsylvania Tunnel (Built by the Pennsylvania Railroad in the early 20th century as part of their construction of an extensive network of rail tunnels throughout the City, including the vital one under the Hudson River as the main connection to New Jersey).

"Just before the River swings to the right is the Williamsburg Bridge, opened in 1903. Whoops! I meant to say, 'to the starboard.' That's right isn't it, Lou?"

"Right on, Nico. Now you sound authentically nautical, my dear," called out Lou, while keeping his attention forward as they headed for the waters of the Hudson.

"For many years," carried on Nicole, "the Willamsburg was the longest suspension bridge in the country. The record fell in 1924 to the Bear Mountain bridge, up the Hudson some distance north of the City. The Williamsburg also carries a subway line as well as automobiles into Brooklyn.

"Next comes the Manhattan Bridge. It was also opened in 1909, but in December, about nine months after the Queensboro. Those were busy bridge building years. The Manhattan bridge also connects automobiles and the subway into downtown Brooklyn.

"The last bridge, but actually the first to be built across the East River, is the famous Brooklyn Bridge, opened for auto and pedestrian traffic in 1883. It was designed by Augustus Roebling (pioneer in the fabrication of steel cables, which he successfully used in the construction of suspension bridges). Due to his untimely death, the work was completed by his son. The Brooklyn Bridge is incredibly sturdy. According to technical estimates, it was built some six times stronger than needed, and should serve indefinitely. Furthermore, it was the longest suspension bridge in the world at the time—a credit to Roebling's engineering prowess. Also the Gothic architectural design of the Brooklyn Bridge continues to be widely admired."

Oscar chuckled, cleared his pipe by tapping it bowl-down over the side of the boat, and said, "Very interesting, Nicole. You could qualify as a professional river guide. And I'm sure you have more to tell as we turn around Manhattan for the return cruise up the Hudson."

"You're right on the money, Oscar. But between the two of us though, I wouldn't want the job. Thanks for your generous comments anyway. Before we leave the East river, I mustn't overlook a major tunnel connecting the lower end of Manhattan with Brooklyn. When it opened in 1950, it was called The Brooklyn Battery Tunnel, and enjoyed the designation as the longest continuous vehicular underwater tunnel in North America. In 2010 it became officially known as the, Hugh L. Carey Tunnel, in honor of the Governor of New York State."

Lou slightly slowed the boat as it turned towards the passage between the southern tip of Manhattan and an island off to the port.

Jane, who was still standing, asked, "What's that rather large island called? Frankly I didn't know it existed until now."

Nicole checked her notebook and called out, "It's name is Governors Island and is approximately one-half mile off the tip of Manhattan. It's been upgraded as a park and declared an Historical Landmark District, which people can visit during the summer months on free ferries. During the Colonial period the highly fortified Island strategically commanded the maritime approach to the City.

At that moment, approaching at considerable speed out of the Upper New York Bay, was a very large yacht (undoubtedly private) that abruptly turned into the passage between Manhattan and Governors Islands—just as Lou's boat came down from the other direction. Lou immediately tensed. His first reaction was to turn his boat away. But there wasn't sufficient room to maneuver within the constricted waterway. Both boats were committed. He felt trapped between the land on his starboard and the oncoming boat on his port. Without delay, Lou reduced speed and steered closer to Manhattan (he was following the Marine Rules of the Road: power-boats meeting head on pass port to port, and move to starboard for maximum leeway).

Actually there was ample clearance to safely pass each other, but Lou knew that the impact of the yacht's considerable wake on his much smaller boat would be unsettling. He called out, "Everybody grab hold of a railing for firm support, especially you, Jane. When that big yacht passes we're going to bounce like a cork for a while as its wake washes across our port beam. Damn," Lou angrily shouted out loud, "I wish he would slow down. That monster boat is probably run by some self-centered Wall Street mogul who thinks he owns the City, and acts as if these were his private waterways. Look, the bastards sticking to the middle of the channel without any move to his starboard, nor has there been even a modest reduction in speed. It's inexcusable for that arrogant skipper to ignore boating's traditional courtesy towards other boats. He should be seriously penalized. What we need are police boats patrolling these waters and enforcing speed limits, as some other harbors do. He's not only a bastard but also a fucking, son-of-a-bitch. Unfortunately, the hard reality is that boating enjoys the unusual status as the last refuge of anarchy, and will likely remain uncontrolled. All boats must be State registered, but the owners aren't licensed. To own a boat you simply need the price, and off you go—whether you know anything or not about boat handling."

Jane smiled at Lou's outburst in silent admiration for his outspoken indignation; while Nicole grimaced with anxiety and surprise at Lou's use of profanity. She was alarmed at what sounded like trouble, and instinctively reached out to grab Oscar's arm for security. He had promptly seized the rail on his side with the other hand, while his teeth firmly clamped down on the pipe stem, and seemed unaware of Nicole's arm wrapped tightly around his. Negative thoughts flooded Nicole's mind, *My god, are we in danger once again? Will Lou know what to do?*

As the huge wake rolled towards him, Lou acted decisively: Instead of passively allowing the wake to hit the boat sideways—with tipping and rocking, threatening to topple people—he gunned the engines and turned straight into the wake's crest. The bow rose a bit over the crest and came down with a slap on the other side. The impact of forcefully hitting the wavelike wake at right angles caused the boat to briefly shudder, without anyone losing balance. All together the incident was over in moments, as the boat smoothly cut through. Once into calm water Lou throttled down to a comfortable cruise level, and steered straight through the middle of the now empty passage.

Oscar and Nicole followed Jane's lead: they all clapped and shouted praise for Lou's capable seamanship. Carried away with enthusiasm, Jane leaned over, put her arms around Lou, pulled him firmly to her, kissed Lou on the cheek, and whispered in his ear, "What a great skipper!"

When he felt her body crush into him a wave of physical pleasure was almost staggering. Without any outward show of emotion or response, Lou steadfastly faced towards the bow, forced himself to concentrate on steering with both hands, and struggled with the impulse to reach out and pull Jane back. A subtle smile of pleasure, though, was irrepressible. Lou's heightened erotic response to Jane evoked some discreet reflections, *What a delight. God, I still tingle from the feel of her full soft breasts pressing into my shoulder. I wish she'd hung on longer. Wonder whether she's giving me a sign of encouragement? No way. I'm just fantasizing. Better watch myself. After all . . . I'm supposedly a happily married man, and hope to keep it so. I'll chalk up her surprising embrace to a friendly spontaneous gesture due to the excitement.*

Meanwhile, Nicole, still unsettled and distracted by events, failed to notice Jane's embrace. She had turned to Oscar and was telling him how alarmed she'd been, and how skillfully Lou managed the boat. She topped it off by saying, "Isn't he a natural as a skipper. And Lou just loves the whole boating scene. I'm trying hard to keep up with him.

"Oh, look up ahead," Nicole called out as she turned forward. "There's the towering Statue of Liberty on the small Liberty Island, which since 1886 has dominated the harbor with its incredible magnificence. Just to its right is the larger Ellis Island. I learned that between 1892 and 1954 amazingly over twelve million immigrants entered the United States through that portal. Hard to imagine what it was like. The original immigration station buildings are still intact and now houses a museum. The two-island complex are administered by the National Park Service." She paused, looked at Oscar and Jane, and tentatively questioned, "You said you're interested in hearing my amateurish commentary, but maybe I give too much."

As usual Oscar only smiled and left it up to Jane to respond. "Nicole, darling, you have been most thoughtful. Not only are we enjoying this rare opportunity to ride through the City's waterways, with its totally different and memorable perspective of the City, but you have also entertained and enlightened us. Without exaggerating, we are very grateful, to say the least."

Nicole closed her notebook and smiled with pleasure.

Yet, for Lou, the encounter with the yacht had been a strain. It took him a while to emotionally calm down. He realized his mix of fear and anger were unsettling, and could have been immobilizing. So, he focused his thoughts on the positive—how his last-minute decision to cut into the wake succeeded. He was reassured, and indulged in self-congratulatory musings, *Despite the stress I performed well, never lost control of the boat, and did the right thing. Now where did the idea to cut into the wake come from? I'll think about that. Thankfully it sure worked out O.K.. They say experience is the best teacher. I'll consider myself self-taught. Probably the best way to learn.*

Feeling relaxed, with a perked up outlook, Lou was lost in his own thoughts.

I can't get over how it didn't take me long to master this big ship. Something very satisfying about being responsible and in control of such power, and knowing how to employ it. I love the feel of standing up here on the bridge, commanding an unobstructed view in all directions, with the helm in my hands, poised and confident that I can handle whatever challenges come my way. On the other hand, I guess my usual stomach cramps will continue. They're a small price to pay for the thrills of boating. Hopefully, maybe in time they'll fade out. But, Lou admitted to himself, *My anxiety reactions while boating did tend to make me feel somehow diminished as a skipper.* He was ashamed of what he thought as an unmanly failing, and was determined to keep it a strict secrete even from Nicole, and particularly from Jane.

The turn into the Hudson marked the midpoint in the cruise. Lou turned to Nicole and asked, "What say, hostess. If you're ready, this might be a good time to breakout the chow. I don't know about the rest of you, but I'm starved."

***

"Why, Nicole, you did yourself proud with this tasty lunch," offered Jane, who had sat down to eat. "And, skipper, tell me, aren't we planing now? We must be with the boat so level and it feels like we're just skimming on the surface of the water."

"Ha! Jane, are you sure this is your first boat ride? You're absolutely correct. On this non-turbulent flat water we'll make good time up the Hudson. It seems like my mini lecture this morning registered with you."

Nicole rushed to speak up, "Before Lou launches into some other boring technical monologue, let me tell you about a boating experience we had that's the other side of the coin. Boating isn't necessarily all fun and games, but could be downright dangerous."

Jane and Oscar turned to face Nicole as she told about Hell Gate. Lou didn't say a word and listened attentively. He was impressed how Nicole remembered every detail of the frightening drama. *She was right,* he thought, *their Hell Gate encounter had been truly scary.* Suddenly, without warning, despite the considerable time lapse, Lou vividly relived the experience. The anxiety and fear he felt at the time reawakened with a troubling impact. He shook his head as though to dispel the reaction, and told himself, *Get hold, old buddy, and don't look back. And certainly don't look dreary. Boating is fun, as long as you know what you're doing and exercise proper caution. We don't want to frighten Oscar, and specially Jane, who I got the feeling doesn't frighten easily. Moreover, her enthusiasm for boating is obviously genuine. We must get then back again. To tell the truth, I would love for Jane and I to go cruising together—just the two of us. Who knows what would develop. Oops, that's dangerous thinking again. Yet, I can't help envisioning how delightful it would be for Jane and I to sail off somewhere alone: It's a palpable pipe dream, with her standing next to me on the bridge with an arm tightly around my waist, pressing snugly, and aglow with the joy of boating . . . Best not to even think about such a possibility.*

Both Jane and Oscar were spellbound as they listened to Nicole's horror tale of the Hell Gate experience. Oscar puffed on his pipe with nervous abandon. Gratefully the thick stream of smoke drifted aft away from Lou who couldn't stand its smell. Jane sat transfixed: with eyes stretched wide open, and mouth slightly agape. They were totally caught-up in the story. When Nicole finished, Jane reached across and—with tears of relief running down her face—hugged Nicole tightly and said, "Thank God you got through that safely." While embraced, Nicole gently tapped on Jane's back in acknowledgment of her sympathetic comment and response; then turned to look at Lou, who smiled back and nodded his approval.

"O.K. folks it's time to break out the beer," called Lou, anxious to change the subject and lighten the mood. "Nicole, would you do the honors? I hope you all don't mind drinking from the bottles. If not we do have paper cups."

Oscar piped up for a change by replying, "Bottles are fine with me. That's the way I started drinking beer in college. How about you, Jane?"

"I love bottles," she promptly echoed. "A beer right now will hit the spot."

Everyone was quiet for a while as they sipped the beer and nibbled on pretzels. The beer worked not only to quench thirst, but also soon helped everyone to relax with ready smiles. Nicole and Lou were especially relieved that their guests were enjoying the cruise; and Jane and Oscar were thrilled with the invitation, which turned out to be for them a wonderful adventure into the novel boating world. Lou couldn't resist turning to look at Jane who had stood up again at his side. She was holding onto the railing with both hands, facing forward into the wind, hatless head thrown back, eyes firmly closed, with her long strawberry blond hair freely dancing in the warm breeze . . . she looked tantalizing to Lou. He couldn't help but imagine her posed as in a state of sensual release, and was irresistibly drawn to her. Daring to dream—he conceived of them as lovers. Only Lou didn't say anything. He looked ahead and tried to concentrate on running the boat, despite unsettled and repressed emotions.

There was something about the steady hum of the engines with their harmonic-like growl and gentle vibrations that lulled them into contemplative moods. This was particularly so for Lou, for whom the repetitive sounds were reassuring that all was well with the boat. As they cruised along on the wide expanse of the River, Lou wondered, *did the others, like himself, also experience a sense of privilege? If so,* he speculated, *their feelings were likely burdened with a modicum of guilt.* For Lou, running the boat engendered a relished sense of well-earned privilege coupled with an energizing sense of empowerment. These were heady feelings.

The sun was warm, the river surface calm, and the boat planed smoothly with hardly a bump. By chance the boat was running in a flood tide, which augmented its progress: the river's forceful upstream flow drew the boat along at an increased speed, without changing the throttle settings. (Tidal surges on the Hudson only involved about six feet of the surface water, while the mainstream below always continued its downstream flow. Since the draft of Lou's boat was only a little over three feet it was entirely within the tidal movements, whose impact he therefore anticipated and took into consideration with the appropriate throttle settings.)

Reading from her notebook, Nicole picked up where she left off.

"The Hudson is an impressive river. It drains from the heights of the majestic Adirondack Mountains—which fills the vast northeastern reaches of New York State—cutting a deep canyon down from north to south and on to the Atlantic Ocean, in an improbably straight 'rhumb line' (a steady navigational course or line of bearing)" She stopped reading and asked Lou, "Did I get that right, Lou?"

He turned to face her, nodded and said with a proud smile, "Right on the money. You sounded like an old seafarer, patiently briefing a bunch of landlubbers." They laughed and Jane added, "If you're going to call us names, it'll cost you another beer."

"Nicole, you heard the lady," promptly spoke Lou.

At that point Oscar added, "And while you're at it, I could use a second."

"Might as well make it all around," concluded Lou.

Nicole glowed with satisfaction, and after passing around the bottles of beer, continued. "The Hudson offers boaters a deepwater channel throughout its range, allowing them to connect to the old east/west Erie canal—now named the New York State Barge Canal—and sail on to Buffalo and into Lake Erie."

Lou added, "Someday we hope to take that cruise. Probably after I retire and have time. Actually, if we're really ambitious, we could do the complete circle tour: going through the Great Lakes we sail down the Mississippi, into the Gulf of Mexico, around Florida, and back home up the Intracoastal Waterway."

Jane asked, "How long would it take? I bet most of a summer."

"Don't know much about the details at this point," answered Lou, "but I overheard some boat owners talking. Sounded like a cruise of a lifetime."

Privately it had been a trying day for Nicole, and she was glad that it would soon be over. She had worried about her boating anxieties: *Would my fears be too obvious and upset Lou, as well as cause their guests to wonder?* With a sigh of relief, Nicole felt all had gone well and thought to herself, *Good how I hid my apprehension; and my hostess chores went smoothly as they ate everything with gusto. Also it seems my concerns about how my scenic reports would be received were unfounded. Jane and Oscar clearly appreciated the information, and indicated it made the trip more interesting.* Feeling less tense and more confident, she resumed her commentary, "Let me remind you we are passing over two important engineering marvels that cross the Hudson, only they are right under us. I'm talking about the Lincoln and Holland vehicular Tunnels which connect from New Jersey to Manhattan. I can't get over how they were able to construct these gargantuan projects. It's simply mind boggling. Chronologically, the Holland Tunnel was the first one built, way back in 1927. It links to the southern end of Manhattan directly onto the heavily traveled east/west Canal Street. Some ten years later, in 1937, the Lincoln Tunnel was opened. It conveniently connects in Manhattan at 40th Street, with ready access to the busy midtown theater and restaurant district."

"Now, Nicole, if you wouldn't mind a sort of editorial critique, I want to tell you what we've learned about the tunnels from bitter experience," interjected Jane. "Positively avoid both tunnels, especially the Lincoln, during the hours of commuter travel into or out of the City. Those hours are impossible. The tunnel traffic gets incredibly congested and cars can back-up for miles, with interminably long delays. The only thing that will help is a new third tunnel."

They all nodded agreement and Lou called out, "I'll second that."

Nicole filled the conversational pause by resuming her tour guide ramblings. "You must all be tired of hearing me talk, so for my final report I'll briefly give you some specs on the magnificent George Washington Bridge, just up ahead. It spans from the Palisades in New Jersey to upper Manhattan at 178th Street, into the area known as Washington Heights. When it opened on Oct. 24, 1931, this double-decked suspension bridge earned the title as the longest of its kind in the world at the time. But in 1937 it was surpassed by San Francisco's Golden Gate Bridge. The lower deck on the G.W. Bridge was finally opened for traffic in 1962. As you all know, people now love to refer to the lower deck as the, 'Martha Washington.'

"Despite the evident misogynist tone in naming the lower deck for George's wife Martha, and its predictable male chauvinist appeal," blurted out Jane while restraining her laughter, "I can't help getting a kick out of the name. The mental image it provokes, I admit, is undeniably very clever and quite funny."

Nicole was taken aback by Jane's admission of delight with the name for the lower deck. Her statement seemed to be contradictory and confusing to Nicole.

Lou on the other hand liked Jane's comment. Her bold, and articulate honesty only further increased her appeal.

CHAPTER EIGHT

In his early boating days Lou focused on learning to handle power boats. First a single-engine I/O—which he quickly mastered—then a major move up to a twin-screw cabin cruiser. The challenge of the cruiser was more than anticipated. He soon admitted to himself, *This rascal is not a simple step up, but is more like a quantum leap. Running on open waters was easy. All I had to do was to steer straight, and avoid other boats by following the prescribed Marine Rules of the Road: Such as, when two boats are approaching head-on the Rule calls for them to pass Port to Port, thus safely guiding passage. Otherwise the situation could cause confusion and danger. The Rules are essential and sensible, aimed to prevent collisions, but work only as long as everybody follows them. I worry about novice boaters who are ignorant of the Rules. All they needed was the price of the boat and are free to sail without any licensing requirement or knowledge-based test, which creates a potential danger to themselves and others. But for me, the preeminent challenge was managing to safely steer—at idle speed—*

through a marina filled with other vessels, and then teasing the boat into a berth stern first.

It took Lou considerable time and concentrated study to adequately master the skills for running the cruiser, to where he felt confident and less tense. At first he memorized the many combinations of engine settings, and how the boat responded to each. Then quietly at home, Lou rehearsed all the complex moves until he felt secure in how to instantly respond to the varying conditions he expected to confront. It paid off. He became increasingly pleased with himself as his skill improved. Still, when he observed master skippers at the controls, boatyard technicians in particular who steered twin-screw boats unerringly through the yard's narrow channels to the service dock with casual virtuosity, Lou knew he was an amateur, and would likely never achieve their level of expertise. With patience and with time he gradually improved, and the stomach cramps accordingly diminished.

No one had to lecture Lou about the care and servicing needs of the engines. He knew it was a priority. Marine engines were subject to more stress and hard work than imagined. Pushing a boat through the resistant water put a substantial strain on the engines. It was comparable to continuously driving a car uphill in second gear. Timely and skilled marine engine maintenance was a must for sustained reliable performance.

Surprising as it seems, some folks were cavalier about regular maintenance, even though it was obvious that if the engines failed while on a cruise you couldn't get out and walk to a gas station for help. They assumed if the motors started briskly and sounded good and noisy, then all was well. For boaters who were experienced mechanics, they likely could manage their own repairs—in the dock or out on the water—and always sailed with the necessary tools and supplies on board. For the non-mechanical majority who were simply recreational boaters, they were totally dependent on the help of the (few) widely dispersed service boatyards. During the busy boating season, an appeal to a yard for assistance by a disabled vessel someplace out on the water wasn't enthusiastically received. The yard had mixed feelings: Their response would disrupt repair work in process; but would be exceedingly profitable. It involved sending a vessel and crew out to locate the boat—not necessarily a quick joyride—with the unwelcome prospects of having to tow it in. Their response was hesitant because it meant that current repair work would be interrupted in order for one of their limited number of mechanics to go out on the job. For the folks on the dead-in-the-water boat, the interminable delay for assistance was frustrating. In due course, the yard's charges were predictably exorbitant.

The so-called 'proportional' expense of the rescue operation was defended on the basis of the time, manpower, and equipment involved—and rightly so. Trapped by circumstances, the boat owner had no choice but to pay up. Costs are not over. Now the failed engine(s) must be repaired. If the engine(s) were old or of an unusual make, then the rare parts would have to be ordered, prolonging the repair indefinitely. Yes, boating is costly. Even the wise monkey understood this as he peed in the cash register and said, "This is going to run into money." And of course, the bigger the boat the more the money.

Generally, boat repairs can be a major time consuming undertaking. Also expect that the yards show no favorites and everyone waits their turn. Which means that the rich guy with a huge yacht will have to wait while they repair, for instance, an outboard motor on a fisherman's skiff, not much bigger than the yacht's dinghy. In areas of the country with short boating seasons, boats are rushed into the water, crowd the marinas and waterways, while exposing them to increased risk of damage to hulls and props in particular, by collision with spring run-off debris. It doesn't take long for the boatyards to become overwhelmed by urgent requests for repairs and service. Thus anticipate that delay could pile onto delay. On top of all this, hapless skippers and their guests could find themselves with a broken boat, tied-up in a strange boatyard many miles from their home port. The inescapably long delays for repair could take more time than anticipated, and might conflict with prior critically important commitments back home, not amenable to easy rescheduling. Thus, people, especially guests, might choose to leave their boat and find alternative transportation home. With boatyards located on the water in out-of-the-way places, convenient land transportation is often unavailable. Inevitably, expensive and inconvenient combinations of taxi, bus, car rental, train, or even airplane have to be arranged. For the return trip to reclaim the boat, the improvised transportation network that served to get home must now be repeated in reverse—increasing the expense and deepening exasperation.

Therefore, keeping the engines in prime operating condition was essential. Preventive maintenance avoids unnecessary down-time, saves a bundle of money, and helps to reduce boat-related aggravation and stress to a minimum.

***

For a while in the beginning, all of Lou's boating was local, where there weren't any navigational concerns. Running up and down the Hudson and around Manhattan were easy: Land formations and structures were within sight and familiar. Lou could enjoy the scenery and relax. It was as though he were driving a car on well-known roads. All he needed to safely sail his boat were nautical charts and the boat's indispensable depth finder. The time did come when he was eager to cruise beyond these secure waters into the expansive Long Island Sound, and maybe even further. He recognized that sailing out there without a navigational device was unwise, particularly with the powerful Atlantic Ocean's fierce tidal impact on the Sound. Moreover, finding one's way to a particular port-of-call by "dead" reckoning—eyeball fixes—alone would be difficult and unpredictable at best. On one hand Lou looked forward to cruising the Sound, but on the other he viewed those big waters with a measure of concern. Furthermore, getting lost out there seemed a real threat. But he was uncertain what navigational instruments were available, and needed some guidance in the choice of one.

The answer was readily forthcoming when he made inquiries around the marina. The responses were totally consistent: Every skipper he asked had a 'Loran-C.'—widely available for civilian use by 1958. They all agreed that it was the essential navigational instrument. Everyone swore by it, and said they wouldn't want to go far from the marina without a Loran. Lou promptly bought one and had it installed. His boat now sported two antennas: one for his marine radio—which came with the boat as an essential extra—and the new one for the Loran. Lou assumed the name, Loran, was for its inventor, or maybe it was the name of a 'special' woman. Actually, he soon learned, it was an acronym, formed from 'Long Range Navigation,' a technology developed by the United States during World War II. When put into operation in 1943 it proved to be an invaluable navigational system. He chuckled to himself, *Amazing how little I know about boats. But fortunately I'm a quick learner.*

After the technician finished the Loran installation, gathered his tools, and was leaving, he softly mumbled in passing, "I got ya all hooked up. Now all ya have to do is get it tuned-in and ya can start programming your waypoints. There's nothing to it. Just follow the instructions in the manual." And he was gone.

Surprised and uncertain about what that was all about, Lou mumbled, "Waypoints? And they need programming? And I'm supposed to tune the damn thing?" After a few moments hesitation, he walked down the long dock from his ship to have a talk with Tony, the dockmaster, in his little hut at the gas dock. The old hand reportedly knew everything about boating, and Lou needed info about the Loran.

Tony always wore a Greek fisherman's cap, originally white, whose current dirty brown color and spotted black grease stains told of long use. Though his clothes were old and weather-worn, they had a fresh laundered look with a pleasant detergent aroma. His heavy black mustaches hung down on both sides of his wide mouth, and combined with penetrating dark brown eyes he could appear intimidating, and some thought even angry. A sturdy physique packed into a five foot eight inches frame along with unlimited vigor made it difficult to judge his age. And though his rough speech lacked a foreign accent, it was generally assumed he was Italian, even born there, and to the more imaginative, most likely in mafia-overridden Sicily. Marina members were deferential in their dealings with him as though he was in charge, instead of their employee.

In an attempt to broach the encounter in a friendly manner, Lou approached Tony with a wide smile and remarked, "Looks like a good sailing day, eh, Tony?"

Tony turned to face him, looked up at the sky, and without a change in his expression grunted with his deep bass voice, "You'd best not go far out. There's going to be a good blow coming real fast. It'll probably reach 25-30 mph when it gets here. I've already got the small craft advisory flag ready to hoist." He then turned back to his paperwork.

Lou wondered how Tony could so assuredly predict the weather, but decided to stick to his original intention and ask about the Loran system. "Actually, Tony, I was hoping you'd have the time to explain how my new Loran works."

Tony swiveled on his chair, tipped his hat back, and looked attentive. He nodded up and down a few times as his eyes lit up with interest that seemed to cast a glow on his pale olive colored skin. Without so much as a few words of intro, he began talking. "Back during the big war, in the early 40s, the U.S. developed Loran. It gave maritime shipping and the military critical navigational help within an accuracy of maybe 50 feet, and with an approximate range of up to 1,200 miles. Without a doubt I believe the Loran won the war, hands down. If we didn't have Loran all those young landlubbers and hayseed punks put in charge of the boats and planes would probably still be wandering around out there lost, God knows where." Tony paused from his rapid monologue, as if to catch his breath and refocus.

Lou stood a few feet away, frozen in place, trying not to move so as not to distract Tony, who promptly resumed.

"It was a big project. The government built an entirely new radio transmitting network around the country, along the entire coastline. Loran is a terrestrial radio navigational system, which continuously operates sending low frequency signals. During the war, ships and planes had special receivers installed that were programmed to simultaneously accept the signals from three area-specific transmitters. These clever receivers recorded the arrival time of each signal, and noted their differences. Then the receiver pinpointed your exact location with some very clever mathematical triangulation calculations. Amazing. Couldn't have won the war without it," Tony repeated for emphasis.

He stopped again, and a wistful look took hold. Lou impulsively said, "Tony, you sound like you were there."

"Hell! Sure I was. I spent many long years out on the Atlantic in an old rusty destroyer long overdue for the scrap heap. Our main job was to shepherd convoys loaded with the essential supplies for our troops and Allies. But we were heavily loaded with sub-bustin' depth charges. Just exploding one of those cans near a sub was enough to tear it apart. That's all we talked about: hoping to detect one so we could blast them to hell." Tony took a deep breath, and his eyes shifted focus somewhere off into the distance. It was as though he forgot Lou was there.

"Our Captain, a young punk out of Princeton, or maybe Harvard," Tony resumed, "called me into his cabin when I first arrived, and said, 'Seaman, we need a navigator. You look smart, so here's the manuals and this new gadget called a Loran. I'll depend on you to get us where were going.' I knew shit about navigation," loudly interjected Tony, "but I learned fast enough. I was just a kid myself, eager to impress and do my part. Best of all as navigator I had a dry place inside during those many crossings, and didn't pull outside duty. Regardless of the weather, in storms and such, there always was a team standing alongside our depth charges, ready for an immediate response if one of them Kraut subs showed up. The subs were on the prowl for merchant ships, so we were told they didn't waste torpedoes on us, thank God.

"Nonetheless, I was never relaxed. I expected at any time to be blown to bits without notice.

"Our Navy did its best with the few ships we had to guard long lines of slow-moving overloaded freighters strung out over a wide area. Naturally we had to reduce speed to match the slowest in the group, making us easier targets. In the early years, the subs had no trouble picking off more than one unlucky ship on every trip. I still have nightmares recalling those sudden explosions as a torpedo hit, followed by billowing black smoke marking the dreadful spot. I almost shit myself each time. Seldom did any crew survive. We routinely circled back looking for survivors. All we usually found were plenty of dead bodies floating in their life preservers covered in black oil. The Skipper gave orders to pick them up. A grisly detail which caused some of the guys to upchuck. After a while, the dead bodies became a gruesome reality, strangely part of our routine. No one talked about it or upchucked any more. On the surface we had adjusted and seemingly handled it with dispassion. But let me tell you, images of those awful bodies, some torn horribly apart and all reeking of oil, fill my nightly dreams. I swear I can still smell the oil.

"I was surprised at how little remained of the ships. Many were old hulks, loaded to the brim. They split and sunk quickly. Some carried ammunition of all kinds, including incendiaries and heavy bombs, whose explosion added incredibly to the noise and fury caused by the torpedo. We got so that when one of those were hit we knew it was an ammo ship by the series of additional explosions. Sometimes the explosions continued after the ship had sunk. The crew had no chance to survive such cataclysm.

"But, don't you worry, we balanced the scales by sinking a few of their subs in return. On one occasion a damaged sub came to the surface shortly after a big oil slick appeared. Slicks usually meant we hit it bad. A white flag of surrender was immediately mounted on the conning tower. We all shouted with joy. It wasn't often we got lucky. The depth charge crew were the heroes of the day after closely targeting them with a dozen cans. We pulled over to pick up the crew who were all jumping into the water cause the damn sub started to sink fast. Our boat barely had room for them, and we didn't have nothing like a brig. But they were grateful to be alive and gave us no trouble. A surprising number spoke English and translated orders to the rest. Our Skipper put them all to work. He told them they had to earn their keep. I admit the boat looked a lot better after a while with much of the rust scraped off and the heads cleaner than ever. At first I wondered why we saved those killers. My attitude modified with time as we interacted with them. For the most part they seemed to be just a bunch of scared kids . . . like us. Of course, maybe their Captain and officers were a bunch of Nazis."

Tony and Lou were both still for a while. Tony looked distracted, lost in memories that weighed heavily. Lou broke the silence by saying, "Tony, thanks for the info on the Loran, and especially for sharing your war experiences with me. You brought those days back so vividly that I could almost feel what it was like."

Tony turned slowly towards Lou, and his usual gruff expression was replaced with a sad, mournful look, so unlike him. His brusque, impatient manner was gone. Lou quietly puzzled at the changes.

Tony slowly regained a measure of composure and in a soft, gentle voice quietly said, "Those days are always with me, day and night. It is like a dark curtain through which I view the world around me. Do you think it'll ever fade?" It wasn't a question, but a lament about his expectations for the future. Curiously he started to wring his hands with a nervous intensity, and said, "I tried alcohol for a time, but it made me feel worse. My first wife gave up on me. She couldn't deal with my drinking and nightly screams, so left. For a while my life almost went over the cliff. When I met Lorelei, a nurse in a vet hospital where I was drying out from one of my worst alcohol binges, my life brightened up. For reasons I can't understand, she took to me, and helped turn me around. She won't marry me, but we have been living together for some years now. If there's a god in heaven, then she's the guardian angel he sent to look after me." He stopped talking, looked down as though embarrassed, and after an awkward moment added, "Sorry about all that. It's rare, but sometimes I can't help spilling my guts out."

Lou was stunned by Tony's revelations, and was momentarily speechless. Finally he offered, "Tony, it's O.K.. Once in a while we all need to let our personal demons loose. It's supposed to make you feel better. I'm honored that you allowed me to listen."

At first Tony didn't reply. Then he stood up from his seat, nodded up and down, and reached out to shake Lou's hand. Surprised by their emotional involvement, they were reluctant to end the contact. Their firm clasp lasted.

As Lou turned to go, Tony said, "By the way, enjoy the Loran while you can. Within the near future it'll be replaced with a new technology called GPS—Global Positioning System. It's supposed to be a space-based satellite navigational system."

"What," cried out Lou. "I'm barely into Loran and you tell me it's almost passé."

Tony chuckled and added, "Hold onto your hat, Lou, things are changing fast. It'll take a few years before we can use it, I suspect. Once again, the US Department of Defense developed the GPS as an improved navigational system." *(Tony knew what he was talking about. GPS became fully operational for the military in 1995. By 2000 it had spread to civilian use and became so popular that it replaced Loran, which ceased operation in 2010.)*

CHAPTER NINE

Nicole was annoyed that Lou had been gone so long. She couldn't help wonder, *what was he up to?* Relieved to see him finally return, she watched as he slowly strolled back, looking subdued and thoughtful. Then when he climbed back onto their boat without a greeting, she concluded that something upsetting had transpired. She intentionally breathed deeply a few times to calm herself before she asked, "Lou dear, is there something wrong? You look so sad."

A wan smile was all he could muster. He hesitated, as though trying to refocus before finally answering, "You know, I just learned that one should never judge a person by appearances alone. It's an old cliché that painfully has to be relearned now and again. Tony surprised me. We had a remarkable discussion. Actually, once he started talking all I did was listen. I never could have imagined that he would be so open about himself, including his troubled life. He said some incredible things. Nicole, I'm sorry but I'd rather not go any further into it right now. Later, after I've had time to digest what was said, I'll happily share his story with you."

"I was worried about you and especially concerned that you looked so upset," said Nicole.

Lou answered with a broad reassuring smile, "I'm fine, just thoughtful. However, Tony was happy to explain a lot of basic Loran system stuff, which after all is what I asked about. So if you're up to it, let's try to tune it in and make the damn thing work. Here's the manual. You slowly read the instructions out loud, and I'll press the buttons."

Nicole was glad for the subject change, hoped it would work to brighten his spirits, and said, "I'd be delighted." She thought to herself, *How nice that he asked me to help for a change. Most of the time he's busy with something-or-other on the boat while I'm off to the side with a book.*

After slowly reading the manual for only a few minutes, Nicole broke into explosive laughter. Through joyful tears she finally was able to explain, "I can't do this. It all sounds like Greek to me. Or should I say Japanese. I don't understand a word of what I read." Her laughter was contagious and Lou couldn't help joining in.

Without explanation, Lou surmised that the highly technical language had provoked Nicole's mirthful outburst. He couldn't blame her, and wondered, *Would I be able to make sense out of the directions and follow them? Furthermore, the well-intentioned Japanese author of the manual hadn't quite mastered the translation into acceptable colloquial English, and wrote in a stilted awkward way, which combined with the technical material, proved more confusing than need be.*

"Ah, the hell with it for now," Lou exclaimed. "Don't worry. I'll give it a try some other time. There's no rush. Let's enjoy the day and cruise up to Croton, anchor, and have a leisurely lunch."

***

From the craggy northern highlands in Eastern New York State an awesome canyon runs north to south down into the Atlantic Ocean. The canyon was believed to have been cut by the mighty cataracts of the Hudson River, through which the River flows abundantly as ever before. This continuous deluge of water from the River serves the Ocean's unquenchable thirst, with little apparent impact. It is one of nature's spectacular oceanographic creations. The unspoiled beauty of the Valley is dazzling. Visitors are delighted and surprised to discover that the Hudson Valley's verdant hillsides overlooking the River throughout its drainage locale still appears to be essentially unchanged—much as they were when Henry Hudson sailed up the River in 1609, reportedly as far north to what is now Albany. Though the encroachment of contemporary constructions dot the landscape—bridges most conspicuously—their presence is overshadowed by the River's grandeur, with cliffs and highlands all adorned with nature's unrestrained exuberant growth of vegetation. Accordingly the Valley's undiminished pristine splendor will likely endure to amaze and enrich countless generations to come.

Henry Hudson, an English sea captain and navigator, was in the employ of the Dutch East India Company when he made his historic voyages. Those bold explorations were the basis for the Netherland's claim of sovereignty over the River, its bordering lands, and (of explicit commercial interest) the many deepwater harbor sites sheltered within the junction of the Hudson River and the Atlantic Ocean. The Dutch promptly announced the establishment of a colony, called the New Netherlands. In 1624 settlers from Holland arrived on the southern end of a large island in the harbor (now known as Manhattan Island) which marked the founding of the colony's capital city, fittingly named New Amsterdam.

Some 40 years later, in 1664, a British military force under the Duke of York—the King's brother—conquered the city, and renamed it New York City. England's extensive coastal holdings were thus expanded and consolidated. The English then decreed the annexation of vast regions of the unexplored hinterland, and designated it as the Province of New York. Those were the years of aggressive and competitive empire building (an euphemism for military conquest) by the major European nations.

Nonetheless, the permanent impact of the Dutch throughout the region is still evident by the survival of many Dutch place-names, and by the large number of people in the Valley who trace their heritage to those migrants from Holland. The Dutch came early to the 'New World' with hopes and dreams for a better life—as did many other groups in subsequent times—and found in the Hudson Valley a land closer to a 'Garden of Eden' than they could have imagined. Moreover, many Dutch entrepreneurs are credited with the establishment of a series of posts, towns, and forts along the River which laid the groundwork for towns and cities that exist today.

***

"That was easy," said Lou as the anchor solidly bit into the River bottom. "We have a good hold here in the shallow (eight to ten feet deep) waters of Croton Bay. Maybe it's not a true marine bay, but an overly-wide recess off the Hudson's main stream, more likely a cove. Nicole, notice how that narrow finger of land on the Bay's southern border boldly projects out into the River. It's called the Croton Point Park, and effectively helps to shelter the Bay from the forces of the Hudson's strong tidal currents, creating a popular placid anchorage for boaters. I understand the Bay is usually filled with boats on many a weekend and predictably on holidays. People swim, sunbathe, indulge in onboard festive picnics, consume (perhaps) a fair amount of beer, and socialize with friends by rafting (tying) boats together. Some people in the marina facetiously delight in calling the Bay 'the Riviera on the Hudson.' My marine charts of the Hudson Valley are invaluable. Without them I would hesitate to ever leave the marina. Besides providing essential information of safe boating channels with water depths and locations of hazardous underwater obstacles, they offer interesting geographic data. For instance, the expansive, three-mile wide Haverstraw Bay—bounded on the west by the town of Haverstraw with its sizable busy marina, and on the southeast by Croton Bay—is distinctly the widest location on the River. And of course from our point of view, the brief 15-mile cruise upstream from our marina to the Bay adds to its appeal. Can't beat this place. Can we?"

"Lou, you're absolutely right. This is the kind of boating I like. Croton Bay is my favorite. No waves or ugly whirlpools, shallow depth, and close to home. So sit back and let me set up our lunch. Today we're going to have your special: bagels and cream cheese with thin slices of Nova Scotia salmon, and washed down with a mug of strong

Columbian coffee. And to top it off, I picked up a delicious rum cake for dessert."

Just as Nicole was slicing the cake, the sudden sound of a group of people cheering reverberated across the Bay. Lou and Nicole stood up and looked around to see what was up. At first nothing unusual was seen. The sounds were mixed with laughter, so there was no cause for alarm. The cheering increased as the response spread among the many boats, and were accompanied by clapping and whistling. Lou soon located the source of the uproar by following the direction people were looking. In a small boat that had stopped on the inland periphery of the Bay, drawn up close to the many anchored boats, a young woman was standing up, her hands held high, naked to the waist, with a broad smile of delight illuminating her pretty face as she turned slowly back and forth. Lou was startled at the surprising display and couldn't help but think, *Damn, what lovely breasts. They are full, not too big, and if I'm not mistaken her nipples are standing up as though she were sexually aroused. Can't imagine what provoked her behavior. Maybe she's on some drug or other.*

At that moment Nicole uttered, "What are these young people coming to? She must have read about the nude beaches in Europe and decided she'd start a trend here."

Lou laughed and said, "Not a bad idea at that. Got to give her credit for the courage, though should I say the boldness, to pull such a stunt. Oh well, let's get back to the cake. The lunch was a treat, Nicole, and especially the rum cake. I don't know why, but I never get tired of it."

***

The typical powerboat has a shallow draft hull design, that paradoxically is its 'Achilles heel.' These hull configurations allow boats to plane at high speeds going straight ahead. Yet it takes very little pressure from wind or current to push a powerboat sideways. Planing ability is not limited to small boats. Moderate-sized boats with appropriate hull designs, with twin screws for instance, will lift up to plane and skim across the water. Even huge yachts with drafts of only a few feet could be pushed sideways by a youngster. Therefore, these shallow draft and planing hulls were very vulnerable to the vagaries of winds and currents. When such powerboats were struck sideways by winds or rushing currents they were easily deflected from their course. Owners of sailboats enjoy pointing out how the deep keels on their boats prevents any sideslipping. Furthermore, they boast how sailboats harness the wind to drive the boat, while instead, the wind causes powerboaters concern and difficulty. Of course powerboaters have a come back. They emphasize that they are not dependent on the wind, and can cruise (almost) regardless of the weather. It probably all boils down to whether one is a wind or gas junky.

***

On the return trip to the marina the weather suddenly changed, as does happen. The warm sunny day faded, replaced by a cooling shade. A rapidly moving cloud cover blocked the sun, while moisture-laden heavy black clouds that threaten rain were absent. However, the unwelcome increase in the wind's velocity did worry Lou. He noted how the wind had accelerated the movement of the clouds, and knew his boat was also subject to the same relentless force. He feared that the boat's handling would become considerably more difficult as the winds increased in power. It didn't take long for him to feel the pressure building in the helm. The boat was tending to slip to port. Repeated steering corrections and mildly beefing up the engines helped somewhat to offset course disruptions caused by the strong gusts out of the west which thrust against the boat on the starboard side. While coming down the spacious river, he had more than ample room to maneuver. His two big engines were a comfort. They could easily counter whatever nature threw at him.

But worry he did, when he envisaged the approaching turn into the marina, where the engines would be reduced to idle speeds. *It wasn't reassuring,* he thought, *that my previous dockings had gone reasonably well. On all those occasions the winds were gentle or lacking and the currents sluggish, so managing the boat was all I had to deal with. Now it's different. The powerful winds and racing tide have changed the entire balance of forces, and maybe it'll be too much for me to handle. How the hell did I ever get into this fix?*

As he neared the marina's entrance Lou looked up at the flag on the roof of the dockmaster's hut. He wasn't surprised to see it strung out horizontally by the wind pointing due east. But with disturbing frequency the flag moved back and forth—from east it shifted to pointing somewhere between south and southeast, and then rapidly rotated back to east. This shifting of the gusty wind was not a welcome sight. Moreover, Lou didn't need the fast-spinning wind gauge, also on the rooftop, to tell him that the velocity was considerable, nor that the speed seemed to be increasing. He feared the building wind. It might reach what were the dangerous small craft warning velocities of 25 to 38 mph. The steering interference created by the wind was clearly substantial. On that day, the surging flood currents streaming through the marina were another. *If I had only known beforehand of the potential weather change, I would have stayed in the marina.* He mumbled to himself, *It's about time I took a course in weather and learned what it was all about. But it's too late for hind sight, and now I have a challenge I would have gladly avoided.*

As the old stomach cramps took hold, he wondered if he would be able to cope with the stress. What he didn't need was for the cramps to worsen, to where he could actually soil himself. *OK, now keep a tight asshole whatever you do, and especially remember not to trust a fart,* he warned himself. Despite the cool air, Lou was sweating profusely with the moisture running down the inside of his arms. His anxiety had increased to an unsettling near-panic state, against which he braced himself and stoically carried on. He had no choice. It was all up to him. Filled with misgivings he turned the boat into the marina's entrance, reviewed for the last time what to do, and then aggressively executed all the right moves: he reduced the engines to idle speeds; released his 'death grip' on the helm; and positioned his hands over the four engine control levers with which he would steer and guide the boat. *That a boy*, he said to himself, *You did well so far. Now comes the damned ball-busting part.* Resisting an impulse to slow or even stop the boat, he maintained idle speed since some headway was essential for control of the boat. Lou made minor lever adjustments as the boat slowly moved down the marina's channel between rows of berthed boats. Despite his best efforts he couldn't keep the boat centered in the channel, and noted with dismay that it was slipping more and more to port—getting too close to the boats on that side.

He was totally absorbed in managing the boat so that all the usual surrounding sounds and sights were blocked. Lou stood tall on the bridge with a focus of rare intensity. The situation was high-stakes—entangled with awful weather over which he had no control. Doubts that he could muddle through, nearly immobilized him. Actually, most people in the marina had stopped whatever they were doing to watch Lou's struggle to safely dock. They knew he was a novice, and not only worried about him, but also were realistically concerned that he might crash into their boats. Silently everyone gazed with rapt attention at the unfolding, intense, and exciting drama—lost in their own thoughts. The experienced boaters couldn't help but conjure up lever moves that would help Lou. Others were reminded of their own terrified early days at the helm. For some the déjà vu emotions were disturbing.

Lou's boat finally came abreast of his slip on the starboard. With an inner sigh of relief, he stopped the forward motion of the boat in preparation for backing into the slip. Next he warily spun the boat port-wise, to line up the stern perpendicular to his dock. While turning the boat, with his eyes focused aft, Lou was unaware how closely his bow had come to smashing into the bow of a berthed boat in front of him. The owner of the berthed boat had looked away, and then sighed audibly at the near miss. Poised sideways in the channel ready for backing up, Lou's boat was now maximally exposed to both the pressure of the flood tide, and the unrelenting battering by the strong winds.

Tension throughout the marina was almost palpable, as the real possibility increased that Lou might lose control of the boat and drift precariously. Fraught with alarm and uncertainty about the corrective control settings to use, Lou momentarily hesitated (instead of immediately backing before the boat drifted too far out of position). As beginner's luck would have it, the wind miraculously shifted—blowing hard towards the south, thus countering the force of the tide pushing northward—and the boat stabilized. Lou felt the boat stop slipping, and realized he had a very narrow window of time—brief seconds—to get the boat into his slip. Without faltering, he instantly moved the levers to initiate a cautious backup into the slip. Nicole had earlier left the bridge, hung the rubber fenders over the port and starboard sides, and with a drawn, tense expression clouding her lovely face was standing aft, with the mooring lines gripped white-knuckled in her hand.

The backing went smoothly. Except the forces of nature were against him, and prevented the boat from coming close enough to the finger dock on the starboard to allow Nicole to jump onto the dock as usual with the lines. With a desperate look of alarm she was about to call out to Lou when she saw Frank and Mike, their dockside neighbors, rushing onto the finger dock. Before they could call out, she drew back her right hand which held the two mooring lines, and threw them with all her might. They caught the lines on the run and pulled the boat into docking position and tied her fast.

Nicole felt faint from all the stress, and allowed herself to slip down onto the deck of the boat. From her seated position she looked up at Lou on the bridge, who was now also seated, and exchanged a forced smile and a thumbs-up wave. He meekly smiled and nodded to her in return. Then suddenly, as though hit with an electric shock, he realized the engines hadn't been turned off. Appalled at his neglect, he thought to himself, "*Better sit still and calm down, old buddy, before I do something else stupid,* Lou mumbled softly. *I sure wouldn't want to go through a day like this again. Maybe this boat thing isn't for me?* After a moments deliberation, he reached across and angrily turned off the engines.

***

Frank and Mike returned to their boats, and the marina resumed its normal hum of activity. It was as though nothing unusual had happened . . . except to Lou and Nicole. For everyone else the show was over. Lou took a while to regain his composure. On top of everything else, he was shocked to see a slight tremor in the hand that turned off the engines. "*Wow*," he said to himself. "*I'm really a bundle of fucking nerves. Not only can't I remember shit, but I feel peculiar.*" His emotional turmoil was indeed at a high pitch. He looked around the marina from his seat on the bridge in a vague daze. On one hand he was much relieved that the docking went safely without mishap, while on the other hand he was totally drained from the incredible stress and gut-wrenching tension of the docking experience. Thinking clearly at the moment was impossible. He was uneasy and strangely distracted. It would take time for Lou's mental and physical homeostasis to regain a measure of normalcy.

***

Later that same day, while hosing down the boat, Lou noticed that Frank was standing nearby. Lou turned the hose off and called out, 'Say, Frank, I want to thank you for helping me dock. You arrived just in time to save my ass."

Frank smiled back, and in a slow, calm voice replied, "Lou, in boating we all find ourselves at risk at times, and are glad to receive help as needed. I just wanted to tell you how impressed I was with your boat handling. It turned into a rough day on the river, and you got caught at the worst possible time coming into the marina. None of us could have done any better."

Lou was stunned and delighted with Frank's generous remarks. At the moment, Lou didn't appreciate how consequential Frank's comment would be in helping him overcome his emotional doldrums. Before he was able to reply, Frank had turned and was walking back to his boat. Lou called out, "Frank, I owe you one. And Mike, too."

Unexpectedly, the day's experiences turned out to profoundly impact Lou, in positive ways. He lost his cocky, nothing-to-it, know-it-all attitude about boat handling—a common novice stage which Lou now understood as unjustified. He shook his head and concluded to himself, *What a jerk I've been.* Having gained a modicum of wisdom, along with a lesson in humility, he was now poised to seriously consider learning the skills and related fundamentals of a competent and knowledgeable skipper. Lou had heard of the United States Power Squadron organization, and that they offered courses in all the wide ranging subjects of boating, with welcome emphasis on preventive safety. He decided to join the local chapter back home. With determination he thought, *The first course I'll take will be about weather. I must learn how to anticipate and interpret developing weather patterns, so I can avoid the near-disastrous trouble I blindly ran into today.*

CHAPTER TEN

"Hi there skipper. How about giving a gal a ride on your classy boat?" Lou heard the woman call out, and assumed she addressed one of his neighbors. He was busy on the bridge polishing the stainless steel railings, and didn't turn to look. Since he learned the term stainless meant what it said—that the steel would stain, only less than regular steel—Lou conscientiously cleaned the railings frequently, using a special agent. The salt-laden Hudson River water along with the ambient saline-rich air created a singularly corrosive environment that damaged many nautical materials, and eventually would eat into the steel railings if left unattended.

It was the familiar sound of the woman's laugh that drew his attention. Lou turned and looked down at his finger dock, and was startled to see Jane standing there. Incredible as it seemed, there she was—the object of his own private erotic fantasies—with her provocative, yet naturally open smile. Though momentarily unable to speak, he quickly recovered and said, " If I do look surprised it's because I don't get many requests for rides, especially from good-looking women." He returned her smile and thought, *Have the gods decided to reward me after nearly scaring me half to death the other day with that dreadful docking? I don't know why or how she got here, but it's more than I could have dreamed up.*

"O.K. lovely lady," he hastened to add with a winsome chuckle, "by all means, please come aboard so we can talk this over."

Jane noticed Lou had turned to glance down the dock, and offered, "If you're looking for Oscar, he's off in Atlanta at a conference. You lucky boy, you've only got me to deal with." Without further ado, Jane swung her leg over the gunwale and hoisted herself aboard. Lou couldn't help notice how her bare legs were tantalizingly revealed when her skirt slid way up. He hadn't turned away. When he lifted his gaze and met her bold knowing smile, he realized she read his thoughts, and seemed to welcome them.

Before Lou could regain his composure, Jane seemed to anticipate his questions, and explained, "Nicole called this morning to invite Oscar and me for another day's outing on the boat. I was happy to accept. During our talk she mentioned you had gone to the marina to do some maintenance work without her. Before we said goodbye I mentioned that since Oscar was away I would probably go to the Big City for some shopping. I hoped you'd still be here in the marina, and couldn't resist surprising you. And of course, I find there's something very appealing about a man with a boat."

Their spontaneous commingled laughter relaxed them even further. Lou, who had been on the bridge throughout, came down the ladder and said, "Welcome aboard, dear Jane. Your timing is perfect. I now have a legitimate reason to stop polishing the bloody railings, wash my hands, and properly greet my guest. You've made my day. What started out as a dreary lonely one, has now become extraordinarily appealing. You know, Jane, you've been on my mind. I'm so glad you showed up today. The weather's perfect for a cruise, and your sharing it is something special."

"Well, I must say, that is the most gracious welcome I've ever received," quickly responded Jane. "If there's any truth to women's intuition, then mine was working overtime when I just knew coming here was the thing to do. I had no doubts you'd be delighted."

Lou paused to calm his beating heart, and tried to appear serious as he looked her over speculatively and finally said, "But, Jane, though you do look ravishing in that lovely linen skirt, sheer silk blouse, white cotton summer jacket, and heeled sandals, they're not suitable for boating."

Never losing her captivating smile, Jane nodded agreement and said, "Lou, you're a rare man to recognize the fabrics. I'm impressed. Another delightful side of you has been revealed. Now, you must also know that women carry these huge purses for a reason. So, like some good little girl scout, I am prepared for all eventualities. It's marvelous how much mine holds. Wait and you'll see me transformed from a svelte lady about town to a sporty looking sailor. I'll be dressed in bright blue and white boating attire, and wearing non slip sneakers. Amazing how it all fit in my bag."

"Jane, you become more amazing by the minute. Now before we sail off, you must earn your way. I need help getting this new darned navigational instrument programmed. It's called a Loran. I'd like you to slowly read the instructions to me, with emphasis on slowly, while I push the proscribed buttons. Don't worry about the sense it makes. Understanding is not required. We'll follow along mechanically, and hope for the best."

With her usual upbeat enthusiasm Jane replied, "Sure thing, skipper. Sounds like something we should be able to handle. Happy to make myself useful." Within a few minutes the Loran was tuned in and operational.

"What do ya know. That was a piece of cake," proclaimed Lou. He then turned to Jane. With an attempt at looking a bit serious, he started to reach for the manual and suddenly stopped. Instead Lou placed his hands on her arms and gently pulled her to him, and said, "Jane you have earned the skipper's gratitude for your invaluable help, which he extends with an official kiss of appreciation." Lou intended a kiss on her cheek, but Jane, who had been watching him with barely blinking eyes, took the initiative—she put her arms on his shoulders, wrapped them around his neck, and leaned against him. With open eye-to-eye contact, she slowly tipped forward with mouth slightly open, and planted a soft moist kiss. Lou was thrilled with her eagerness, and grasped that his feelings were reciprocated and she was a willing partner. Unrestrained he pulled her tightly—pressing them together, full body-to-body.

The embrace was prolonged. Neither one was in a hurry to end it. Finally, flushed and breathing somewhat heavily, Lou reluctantly disengaged and quietly said, "I've wanted to take you in my arms for years, luscious Jane. If you truly read my mind, you must have at least sensed that. But for now I think we must get organized if we're going on a cruise. This trip will be upstream, where I know a secluded spot to anchor and have lunch . . . among other things." She laughed out loud, kissed him on the cheek, and responded, "Sounds appealing, especially the other things," and went into the cabin to change her clothes.

The air was still cool, with a breeze that felt refreshing, while gentle enough to unaffect the stability of powerboats—those tied fast in the marina didn't unpleasantly rock to-and-fro; and those underway on the River weren't deflected from their heading. Boat people looked around as they emerged from their cabins, holding their ubiquitous coffee mugs firmly in hand, inhaled deeply and nodded appreciatively at the lovely weather. Feeling energized they considered plans for the day. Late morning was often a refreshing time, before the sun reached its zenith and heated the air.

***

Lou always ran the boat from the fly bridge (there were a complete duplicate set of controls in the cabin). From up on the bridge he commanded an unobstructed view of boating activity in his vicinity, allowed for easy checking of the sky for weather developments, and the up-high view was invaluable during docking. Besides, Lou enjoyed being outdoors with the fresh smelling sea air blowing in his face as he cruised. Confinement of any kind always made him uneasy. In addition, boating offered the open environment in which he felt free and unencumbered.

When Jane emerged from the cabin, having changed into her boating outfit, the first thing she said was, "Lou, dear, please tell me what to do to help with the boat. It won't take me long to become a real good crew member, since I'm a fast learner. I'm so looking forward to this cruise with you. To be perfectly frank, I'm not sure whether it's the beautiful boat or your handsome good looks that excites me more." Then she laughed and mussed his hair with her hand, enjoying her tease.

Not surprisingly, Jane quickly learned what was expected to help Lou run and dock the boat. No job was too much, and her high spirits and enthusiasm were impressive. Lou couldn't help speculate to himself, *She's a rare woman. The first thing most women did when their husbands died was to sell the darn boat. Jane would probably keep the boat and run it as the sole female skipper in a marina.*

Lou gazed at her admiringly when she joined him on the bridge, and said, "Jane, you look great. As though you've been boating for years. A natural." She stood still with hands on her hips and head coquettishly tipped, while he smilingly appraised her appearance. She was wearing tight-fitting blue shorts which reached mid-calf; a loose pink short sleeved, deeply v-necked cotton shirt draped over the shorts; a thin white cotton sweater hung on her shoulders, and the pair of blue boating sneakers were without socks. Lou was entranced by the way the breeze caught her silky strawberry blonde hair and lifted it to swing freely behind her. He noted how a thin black plastic barrette held the hair away from her face, and contoured dark sunglasses perched high on her head, topped off the fashionable ensemble. She looked to Lou like a model in a glossy boating magazine ad. He also thought, *How titillating that she's braless. I wonder whether she's also without panties?*

With a playful smile, Jane asked, "Skipper, do you think I'll pass muster?"

The question was obviously equivocal, with shades of meaning, which registered with Lou. It was clear to Lou, *she wasn't asking about her crewing skills, or whether she was dressed appropriately. Certainly not. The subtle innuendo could only be a bold declaration of her willing availability.* He was silent for a bit. Nodding in the affirmative while he looked her over with a lascivious grin, he finally answered, "Without a doubt. You are smashing and most devilishly attractive. By comparison, I'm dressed in old clothes and look like a poor cousin." Lou wanted to grab her and crush her to him, but instead exercised restraint, and added, "Best to focus on preparation for our cruise at this time. We need to get ready to move the boat out of the marina as quickly as possible, before my nosey neighbors get too curious. The place might look empty today since it's mid-week, but there's always people around."

***

Frank was retired and practically lived on his boat, was an early riser and couldn't help hearing Jane's call to Lou when she first arrived. Without intending to intrude, he remained in his cabin, except for a brief moment in order to take a quick look at Jane, which confirmed his suspicion that she wasn't his wife. Frank smiled to himself and thought, *Well, my straight-laced- looking neighbor is going to be more entertaining than I assumed. They'll probably take off pretty soon, and I bet my bottom dollar that he'll anchor in a quiet cove for some fun and games. It's sort of like an initiation ritual for new skippers. We all did it in our day. Damn it! Life passes too quickly. Since my wife died I've had a number of women, but it didn't always turn out too well. I remember how great sex used to be. Couldn't get enough. Now the reality is different and disappointing. Is it possible I'm jealous of Lou? He has precious youth and a sexy playmate to romp with. Should I tell him to enjoy life to the fullest while he can? It's so awfully fleeting. Good lord. Such stupid thoughts for an old guy. What I really need is a second cup of strong coffee to get me moving.*

***

Lou slowly guided the boat up the River. Though he felt emotionally stimulated and impatient, he was determined to appear relaxed and nonchalant. It wasn't easy to contain himself with Jane at his side. Actually she was pleasurably pressed up against him with her arm around his waist. He couldn't help think, *Amazing how Jane's so different from Nicole. The contrast is striking. Nicole, never on her own initiative had embraced him like that on the bridge, and likely never would.*

As the boat moved along, Lou now and then glanced at Jane. He saw that her eyes were closed, head tipped back into the air, and her long tresses streamed out in the wind. While one hand held the railing, it was how tightly she hugged him with the other hand that stirred him so deeply. Lou looked longingly and thought, *Though her eyes were closed she was obviously awake. It's as if she has surrendered to the rhythm of the boat's gentle motions and the engines' repetitive harmonic-like drones, also relishing the wind's gentle caresses. She looks like a sea goddess, who has deigned to descend to my humble boat. Hopefully she'll be around long enough for an intimate engagement with a mere mortal, like the ancient gods were want to do..*

Lou was struck by her beauty, and felt caught-up in her irresistible sexual glow. It was as though he reflected, *Maybe her pheromones had been released and filled the air.* He knew he was mesmerized by her powerful ambiance, was aware of his seduction . . . and savored it. At the same time he both marveled and welcomed her aggressive response to him. Additionally, her enthusiastic passion for boating was remarkable and pleased him immensely.

But the exquisite feel of her body against his had become all that mattered. Besides his physical attraction to her, he sensed that something more meaningful might be developing.

Suddenly, an unwelcome guilty quiver intruded. Without hesitation Lou summarily rejected and suppressed the thought. Jane's body with its steady gentle movement dominated all his senses. She held him tight for security and balance . . . but there was more to it. Powerful longings were awakened, which he knew were irresistible. Possessed by the alluring expectations of delight and pleasure, he quietly smiled to himself, and concluded, *How lucky can a guy get. Best not to say a word. Amazing that she also shares my love of boating, with its freedom, power, and exaltation. Could it be that boating also arouses her sexually? What more could I want. I hope she'll love me just a little more than the boat. Ha! Right now I don't want to disrupt her mood. I shouldn't rush it and seem overly eager. But I can't wait to get to the cove.*

***

Anchoring in the cove went smoothly. Theirs was the only vessel there, which heightened the welcome feel of privacy. The cove was modest-sized with room for three cruisers like Lou's, and the narrow inlet sheltered it from the river's strong current and tidal fluctuations which were hardly felt. *A perfect place for lovers to hangout. Now be cool, old buddy, shelve the love stuff for a while, and probably best to first get busy with lunch,* thought Lou.

"I guess it's lunchtime," said Lou cheerfully as they both climbed down from the bridge and entered the spacious cabin. Looking forward as one entered the cabin, there was a large hide-a-bed type of couch, which when opened could accommodate two, on the left. But the main sleeping area was up front in the V-berth—its considerable width almost matched that of the boat's beam (twelve feet six inches), and then tapered to the bow. Two adults could easily cavort in there with room to spare. A fully equipped galley and head with shower were on the left, right after the couch, just before the V-berth. The comfortable eating area on the right resembled a diner restaurant's booth.

Jane was poised just inside the cabin door, which she had quietly closed behind her, and hadn't said a word. Lou turned to look at her, saw her fetching smile, and wasn't surprised when she softly spoke, "Lou, love, let's first tryout that appealing looking V-berth. If I'm not mistaken, we're both hot and bothered, and not with the weather. What we need is some active lovemaking, to work up good appetites of course. I don't imagine you'll have any objection."

As Lou stammered out, “I couldn’t agree with you more,” Jane had dropped her sweater, removed her shirt, and stepped out of her shorts and sneakers to quickly uncover her gorgeous naked body. For a moment Lou relished the sight, and then undressed. They met in the center of the cabin in a violent embrace. Without hesitation or awkwardness, they clinched and kissed with openmouthed lust, entering each other with moist, active, exploring tongues. Jane held him tightly, and with her arms locked around his neck abruptly hoisted herself up to wrap her legs around him. Lou held her firmly in his arms, rapidly turned and with a few steps gently lowered her onto her back on the V-berth bed. Their hunger for each other was overpowering. They instantly coupled in a frenzy of impatience. A glistening film of sweat soon covered their bodies as they repeatedly joined with seemingly unquenchable passion. They were amazingly compatible, with a sensitivity for each other's sexual needs and preferences as though they were lovers of old. And then inevitably, drenched in sweat, sated and weary, with bodies firmly linked as though reluctant to part, they fell into blissful sleep.

***

It was the delicious smell of fresh brewed coffee that brought Jane out of deep slumber. She slipped out of the V-berth, and without a thought about her nakedness, walked over to Lou in the galley, kissed him on the cheek, and went into the head. He was barefoot, only attired in his boating jeans, with their soft, well-worn, baggy look. Jane soon reappeared, searched around on the cabin floor and settled for her cotton shirt. Lou's wide grin as he watched her move about wasn't missed by Jane. She smiled back at him and said, "O.K., lover boy, don't get any ideas. I understand that too much sex can kill, or maybe cause blindness."

"Oh, but what a way to go," countered Lou. With eyes locked on each other, they burst into knowing laughter. A shared and intimate response with inferences that needed no explanation.

Jane soon said, "Lou, we seriously must now consider getting some nourishment, to fuel our smoldering fires. You promised me lunch and now it seems more like breakfast time."

"I'm ahead of you, sexy lady," cheerfully replied Lou. "In addition to a large pot of brewed Columbian coffee, I have already toasted some slices of crunchy whole grain bread. There are assorted jams, or butter if you prefer, and I am ready with eggs, cooked to your specifications."

"I knew there was something appealing about you. I always had a thing for cooks, and thoughtful ones at that," answered Jane. "The coffee smells great and I'll take it in the largest mug you have, *sans* sugar or milk. Eggs will fit the bill, whatever style you like."

Conversation was on hold for a while as they both hungrily concentrated on eating. Finally Jane asked for a coffee refill, pulled her legs up under her, sat back with the mug held by both hands, shook her head in a gesture of wonderment, looked squarely at Lou with a twinkle in her eyes, and said, "Well, aren't we a pair. This has been an incredible day, by all accounts. Without a single doubt more glorious than anything I anticipated. You have taken my breath away." She paused, took a sip of coffee, smiled intimately, and with slow deliberation calmly asked, "Have you given any thought to where we're going with it? By it I mean us, our future plans, if any." She paused again, kept her eyes steadily on Lou, and with an inquisitive expression, waited.

Lou's eye contact didn't waver nor his expression change, but he was taken aback and unprepared for her forthright question and manner. His mind raced to come up with a fitting answer. Above all considerations, he knew deep down that he didn't want to lose her. She waited patiently, sipping the coffee, knowing that she'd surprised him.

After only a few moments had elapsed, though it seemed longer, Lou nodded, smiled, and said, "Jane, you are the most adorable and remarkable women I have ever known. I came to that conclusion the first time I spied you years ago at some social event. Earlier today I privately thanked whatever gods may be for bringing you to me. And now I can't bear the thought of being without you. Please, let's try to work something out. At the moment my emotions are raw and fragile, and I suspect so are yours. We probably need time to adjust to this new reality."

Jane unhesitatingly said, "O.K., Lou. You make good sense, just like a rational male. You're right. That's what we need for now. But before the boating season is over, promise me we'll somehow arrange another cruise . . . like today. Frankly, I'm just a romantic female. At this moment, if you asked, I'd willingly kick it all over, and sail off with you to a new life."

"Sometimes dreams can be made real," quietly said Lou. He reached out and placed a hand on her arm, squeezed tenderly, and added, "Time will tell, my love."

CHAPTER ELEVEN

"Now tell me again, Lou dear, why you wanted to come to the boat today. After all, the weather promises to be nasty. The sky is filled with dark clouds—which even I have learned usually means rain is on its way—the air is downright chilly, and the prediction we heard on the car radio confirms there's going to be a downpour. Doesn't add up to an enjoyable boating day."

Lou smiled, somewhat indulgently, checked the knot on one of the docking lines, and said, "Nicole, you're right about the weather. There's no doubt it will deteriorate and likely turn ghastly. But, since it's not a suitable cruising day, it's a perfect time for working on plotting the Loran waypoints. Last time I was on the boat I figured out how to activate the darn thing. It's ready to go. Now all that remains are for the waypoints to be chosen, locations measured, and programmed in. It's a one-time initial job that will provide ongoing navigational guidance."

"But I thought once you got it started, that was all there was to it. What's this about waypoints?" Nicole was trying hard to sound interested. She sighed to herself and thought,

Given a choice I can think of a lot more things I'd rather do than spend it on the boat on a rainy day. Good thing I brought along a book. He'll likely be busy with the waypoint thing all day.

"Glad you asked," cheerfully answered Lou, pleased with her question. "Once I turn on the activated Loran it will begin to calculate a fix of the boat's location on the water, even our position here in the marina. When the ship leaves the marina and moves along, the Loran will constantly revise the fix. The clever little devil accepts the continuous radio signals from the land placed transmitters and does the reckoning with its own built-in computer. Still, that's only half of the Loran's capability. I now must add the navigational info, so the machine can guide us when we're off cruising.

"The waypoints are physical reference points that are identified in the Loran by latitude and longitude coordinates. A nasty day like this is perfect for me to sit quietly in the cabin with the marine charts and very precisely work out each waypoint. Waypoints must be chosen with care. If I selected one, for instance, located on the other side of an intervening land barrier, we would run aground, since the Loran directs the boat straight to the waypoint. I'm going to select waypoints that will serve wherever we cruise, whether out on the Hudson or in waters beyond. On restricted and winding waterways waypoints will require close spacing, but on open waters they will often be miles apart. As each waypoint's coordinates are determined I'll feed them into the Loran with an assigned requisite number. When a specific waypoint is needed all I have to do is enter its number into the Loran and then the appropriate navigational data will be displayed, such as: the course (or compass) heading to the waypoint; distance to the waypoint; time to reach it; and the current vessel speed. As changes in the ship's speed occurs, along with inescapable drift due to current and wind, the Loran recalculates and the display is revised. Clever, eh? Now we can plan our first trip out to the Long Island Sound."

* * *

"Good lord, Lou, are we really going to go through Hell Gate?" asked an anxious Nicole."The mere thought of that place still alarms me."

"Fear not, love. Look just ahead and there's old terrible Hell Gate. You'll not recognize it today since the waters are calm. I timed our passage to coincide with slack water. Remember, that's the prolonged interval between flood and ebb, when all the turmoil, waves, and whirlpools disappear. Nonetheless, we could easily sail through the worst of Hell Gate powered by our hefty twin screws. It would be like cutting butter with a hot knife. So sit back and take in the new scenery as we wend our way out to the big Sound."

Still worried, Nicole firmly gripped the railing next to her seat on the bridge. Though confident in Lou's judgement and boat handling skills, she found it hard to relax. This trip out to the Sound would be through new passages that seemed complicated to her. In a disquieted state of mind, Nicole imagined encountering many unanticipated dangers. She felt tense, and unable to control the tremor in her voice as she asked, "Are you sure you can find your way? Looks strange and baffling to me. Are there any other dangerous places like Hell Gate?"

Lou turned to Nicole, realized she was uptight, and with a broad smile tried to calm her fears by saying, "Don't give it another moment's thought, Nicole. I studied the chart, memorized the route, and now know these waters like the back of my hand. And of course, Hell Gate is one of a kind. Nothing like it from here on out. It will be smooth going all the way. And I'll call out the new and interesting features as we go along. It's a part of the City that we don't customarily notice as we drive through in our fast-moving cars on crowded highways. I know you're bound to be intrigued. O.K.?"

* * *

"The first thing of interest I want to point out are the two small islands coming up on our port side. They have the unimaginative names of North and South Brother Islands. The North Island once was the site of a hospital, however they are both currently uninhabited and have been designated as restricted wildlife sanctuaries. It's a marvel how the birds and other creatures learned so quickly that no one would disturb them on the Islands. They soon gathered and nested. Undoubtedly their populations have safely grown quite huge. Here, I'll slow down so we can enjoy the many different bird species flying around. Look, there are a few long-legged ones wading in the water along the shallow shore line, looking for something to eat. On our next trip out this way, I'll try to remember to bring my old copy of Peterson's Field Guide to Birds, so we could identify some of them."

Nicole was delighted with this unexpected finding and said, "Oh, I would enjoy that. Who would have thought that wildlife havens like these exist right here in the center of the Big Apple."

"Surprising," said Lou as he nodded in agreement and resumed his tour recital. "Directly opposite on our starboard is the large Riker's Island. That's where New York City has located their main jail complex, which can accommodate a few thousand prisoners at a time. We're sailing straight ahead through the deep, clear, wide passage between Riker's and the Brother Islands. As you can see, there's room for us and even a large freighter if, by chance, one comes along heading into the City.

"Nicole, notice the heavy air traffic passing over us," continued Lou. "These low-flying commercial jets are coming and going from the International La Guardia Airport, located not far away on the Northern shore of Queens, and separated from Riker's Island by a narrow water channel. It's one of the busiest airports in the country, with reported passenger traffic of well over 25 million a year."

Settling down and feeling more relaxed, Nicole said, "Lou, you sure did your homework and learned a lot of interesting stuff. Your forecast about this trip was correct. The city looks so different from our boat. It's sort of like viewing the city's underbelly, where the basic machinery that keeps the place going is located. It's not as majestic as the skyline image of all the high-rise buildings seen, for instance, from the Hudson River, but in some ways it's more complex and fascinating."

Pleased with Nicole's improved mood and her obvious effort to participate, Lou quickly responded, "You got it just right, love. And let me tell you how impressed I was with the metaphor you just used in your descriptive comments. It was quite vivid. No doubt a woman's sensitive view of things always adds an enriched dimension. Good for you."

Lou had made a concerted effort to overcome Nicole's cautious boating attitude. Her smile in response to his flattery and obvious interest along the way, were encouraging signs that perhaps her somewhat jaundiced view of boating was fading. Yet, from the back of his mind, unbidden and unexpectedly, a vision of Jane's passionate enthusiasm for all things boating intruded, which so excited him. The comparison with Nicole's tentative participation was both unfavorable for her and disquieting to Lou. Nonetheless, Lou tried very hard to dismiss thoughts of Jane, and forced himself to make an effort to focus his attention on Nicole. He looked at her with a wide smile, and resumed the guided nautical tour by saying,

"Coming up ahead are two of man's marvelous engineering accomplishments. The first is the Bronx Whitestone Suspension Bridge, which connects Queens on Long Island and the Southern Bronx. It was opened in 1939."

Nicole jumped in and eagerly called out, "Lou, those 1930s were special years. They built many magnificent bridges then. An incredible era. The George Washington was opened in 1931, followed by the Golden Gate in 1937, and now I've learned that the Whitestone was finished in 1939."

"Boy, do you have a good memory," exclaimed Lou. "I really hadn't made the associations and put those dates together like you did." Then with a facetious chuckle he added, "I'll have to add that tidbit to my spiel. Now back to the Whitestone. It quickly became obvious that heavy daily traffic flows, with frequent tie-ups, had become the norm, and was unacceptable. A second bridge was planned. It was constructed just beyond the Whitestone, was named the Throggs Neck Suspension Bridge, and opened to traffic in 1961. As we come out from under the Whitestone you'll see the Throggs Neck's long, graceful, curved span rising high above the water."

"Oh, yes. What a beautiful bridge," said Nicole with a ring of excitement. "It's truly a sight to see. I'm so glad we came this way."

Lou smiled with contentment, altered course to the north into more expansive waters, and pointed to the right as he said, "Next place of interest is the United States Merchant Marine Academy, situated at King's Point, Queens. The Academy's choice water front property is visible on our starboard as we clear the bridges. It's one of five service academies charged with training officers for the Merchant Marine, military, and transportation industries. Actually, I must admit to how uninformed I've been. I never realized there were Merchant Marine Academies until just recently. Pretty stupid of me, eh? And like the Army and Navy Academies, these Marine Academies also provide the Midshipmen a full four-year program leading to a Bachelor of

Science Degree." After a short pause, Lou continued.

"Coming up dead ahead, slightly off our port beam, is the popular City Island, connected to mainland Bronx by a bridge. Let's visit it one of these days. We'll sail there in our boat, and tie-up at a dock opposite one of the restaurants. I know you'd love the place. City Island has the charming look of a small New England fishing village, and has long been a tourist destination. People are drawn by its many seafood restaurants, that offer fresh lobsters, varieties of fish, and the many assorted types of well-liked shellfish."

"Sounds appealing, Lou. I'll look forward to my favorite whole boiled lobster. Something about cracking open all the shells to get at the meat that adds to the fun." She laughed and added, " I know it's a messy job, but an appealing rare treat to use one's hands and fingers."

"Yes, ma'am, that does sound good. We'll plan a trip real soon," answered Lou, as he scanned in all directions and commented, "We timed our trip today just right. With the few boats around we seem to have these waters almost to ourselves. Nicole, look beyond City Island and you'll just make out the much smaller Hart Island. For all practical purposes it's uninhabited. But Hart does have the singular distinction of providing the City with a gravesite for its unknown dead. Current estimates are that through the years over 900,000 individuals have been interred there."

"Lou," called out Nicole. "What's that little red brick building up ahead? Isn't it a strange place to build a house, right in the middle of the water?"

He couldn't help laugh at her naive question. He turned to her and asked, "Nicole, please come up here and stand next to me, so you can see better. That house might be the most important navigational aid in all of these waters." After a moment's hesitation from the security of her seat, Nicole said, "O.K., Lou. Just make sure you're ready to grab me if I lose balance."

Lou reached out to take her hand as she moved the few steps from the bench to the front rail, and answered, "Don't worry, love, I'm here, and besides we're in calm water so no bumps. That little brick structure is the lighthouse for the critical Stepping Stones Light. Right there at the confluence of the East River and the Long Island Sound was the perfect place for the building. See how the waters appear clear and safe on either side of it. Actually nothing could be further from the truth. Mariners sailing here in the long ago past discovered, to their dismay, that unseen under the placid looking water was a deadly rocky reef reaching out, from what is now Queens, to almost the exact middle of the passage. Many a ship had its bottom torn out going over it. Even today, there are some foolish cavalier boaters that don't bother with studying nautical maps or might not even own them. So every season some of them, out of ignorance, pass the Stepping Stones light on the wrong side and destroy their boats."

"Oh, how horrible. If you didn't tell me the difference, I would have also assumed going on either side of Stepping Stones was safe. And if I were at the helm, I could have destroyed our boat on that awful reef."

"As I pointed out some time ago," resumed Lou sounding earnest. "Recreational boating is unfortunately without meaningful rules and regulations. It's anarchy at its worst. The resulting problems are many. Just for example, the recent dramatic increase in inappropriate 'mayday 'calls for help from recreational boaters for avoidable and non-threatening issues has caused the Coast Guard to just about cease responding. A typical problem is running out of fuel. Private boat yards have filled the gap. They will come to the rescue in due time . . . but at significant cost."

With an element of concern in her voice, Nicole asked, "Lou, dear, is that the Ocean were coming into? The waters looks so immense."

"No. We're just now into the Long Island Sound proper. I believe that perhaps it's the best recreational boating area in the country. The Sound extends for some 80 miles, stretching between New England and Long

Island before it connects with the Atlantic Ocean. Also, the Sound is only 20 miles across at its widest, so we're never out of sight of land and can't get lost. Furthermore, the entire area has many well-maintained navigational aids.

"Today we're heading to Greenwich, Connecticut for lunch. It's just across the Connecticut border, not far out into the Sound. Won't take us long. You'll enjoy docking at the water-side restaurant, where a team of boys will help us tie-up. Then after we enjoy our meal, we can stroll around the Village of Greenwich. It's an old Maritime settlement situated on the water, with colonial charm blended with many modern shops. Bring your credit card. There might be something you fancy."

CHAPTER TWELVE

Lou knew why he was restless and distracted. Despite efforts to get Jane out of his mind, thoughts of her dominated his consciousness. Even when he made love to Nicole he found himself envisioning it was Jane in his arms. Above all, he couldn't think of how he was going to contact Jane to plan another day together on the boat. *Maybe Jane will figure something out,* he pondered. *She's a very self-assured gal and quite resourceful. Besides, I know she's just as eager to get together as I am.*

Nicole very perceptively sensed the subtle change in Lou's behavior, and finally was compelled to ask, "Dear, is there something troubling you? You know I'm here to share everything with you: the good and the bad. I've been worried about you. Lately you seem moody and distant. Something must be wrong. Please tell me what's upsetting you."

Lou was taken aback by her question. He was guilelessly unprepared with a cover story, and felt exposed. Yet, he was moved by her overt concern, along with an uncomfortable sense of vulnerability. He asked himself, *After all, who else would worry about me? Nicole's love was precious and invaluable. I better be careful and not put it at risk.*

Still, his mind raced for an acceptable answer as he thought, *Why didn't I anticipate that Nicole would somehow read a change in my behavior. I think she has that uncanny ability to almost read my mind. I wonder whether all women have that ability?* After a hesitant few moments he said, "Well, love, you missed your calling and should have become a 'shrink.' Now I don't want to alarm you, but for a while now I have had urinary difficulties. Not unusual for a middle-aged guy, but I guess it should be looked into. I've been putting off making an appointment for a checkup. Admittedly, I've been anxious at what they might find."

"Oh my, Lou, why didn't you tell me. I think I know what you're talking about. It's likely a prostate problem. You'd be surprised what I've read in those women's magazines that you like to poke fun at. It's amazing how the subjects they now include have changed so dramatically. In the past the emphasis was on how to bake a scrumptious cake, and the importance of always keeping your nose powdered so as to look pretty and attractive for your husband. In recent years the content has matured with serious in-depth articles, such as discussions about female sexuality; breast and uterine cancer; and for mature couples, male prostate complications and even impotence."

"Wow. You probably know more about these things than I do, and I'm glad you questioned me. I've denied the symptoms far too long. It's time to call the doctor."

* * *

After what seemed like exhaustive tests, Lou was informed that he had prostate cancer. Nicole was surprised at how calm Lou seemed. In contrast, she was overwhelmed and burst into uncontrollable sobs and tears at the news. Lou had insisted that he would go alone to the doctor, despite Nicole's offer to join him for necessary support. When he returned from the doctor with the fateful diagnosis, she broke down and irrepressibly cried as she threw herself into his arms. Though it was an appalling diagnosis, Lou not only maintained a calm, untroubled outward demeanor, but also was less upset than he expected. It wasn't a surprise. He largely focused on recovery, and counted on a cure. His usual hardheaded pragmatic approach to life was what he relied on to see him through.

In the ensuing days, Lou often marveled at how one day he was robust, even enjoying a licentious extramarital affair, when almost overnight he became a cancer patient, and his life forever changed. As if in prayer, time and again he said to Nicole, or mumbled to himself, "What a relief to have had that awful cancerous gland totally removed. Good riddance to it. And I'm everlastingly grateful to that skilled and dedicated surgeon who performed masterly, and likely saved my life."

While appearing calm, Lou however was privately struggling with the monumental impact of the cancer. Though at the onset he disregarded the symptoms, he couldn't help suspect that the increasing creep of urinary difficulties were ominous, and likely caused by his prostate. The overriding reality was sobering: Lou assumed there was nothing he nor anyone else could do to interfere with a malignant growth, short of cutting it out. Furthermore, Lou had long anticipated he would develop prostate cancer. He figured it was only a matter of time, since he suspected cancer had been fatefully programmed into his DNA at the moment of conception.

But for Nicole's sake, he never shared this information with her. From the day he heard the diagnosis he worked hard to shield her from his unceasing burden of tension and anxiety.

The day of his exam by the Urological Surgeon was the turning point. Following the doctor's clinical digital exam, he nodded knowingly and ordered an impressive array of various sophisticated tests. It didn't take long for test results to confirm that he had prostate cancer. In a rather dispassionate manner Lou was told he was a candidate for radical prostatectomy (surgical removal of the entire prostate). He calmly absorbed the news and urged the Doctor to schedule the operation as soon as possible.

Having survived the lengthy surgery, Lou rejoiced at the prospects of a healthy future. His retelling of the cancer saga was irresistible, albeit both gratifying and painful, while satisfying a deep, compelling, emotional need.

* * *

And Lou reflected to himself, *At first I witlessly ignored the un-expected sense of an increased urgency to urinate. I thought (more likely hoped) it would soon pass. But as time went on and the symptom became more demanding, I had to accept its grim implications, and sought medical help. Strangely—but maybe not—an experience from long ago, had come to mind. I was only about ten-years-old at the time, and I'm amazed that the details are still so fresh:*

I was in a men's room at a restaurant standing over a trough-like urinal alongside my elderly Grandfather. Suddenly Grandpa said, "Now listen, Lou. It's time you learned that when you get old peeing changes. Notice how long it took me to pass my water. You, on the other hand, whipped out your pecker and promptly peed away. Sometimes I feel like I must immediately pee, but when I get to the toilet the water won't come out. When that happens I usually have mounting back pain until the flow finally begins. The doctor told me that many old guys have the same problem, and that I must have surgery, real soon. Thought it's time for you to know about this stuff."

Like it was yesterday, I recall how Grandpa's serious talk about this adult male issue, made me feel so grownup. Naturally I had nothing to contribute to that discussion while I eagerly listened. It was a truly unexpected and immeasurably uplifting moment. I still wonder why he considered me mature enough to handle such a heavy subject, and what prompted him to bring it up at all. Obviously, it had a profound impact on me, which I never forgot. In actual fact, as circumstances worked out, Grandpa's tale accurately portended my prostate future.

I wonder whether my father had the same problem, and now it's my turn? The 'genes will out,' they say. No doubt about that. If we only had the option to check the health histories, including longevity expectations of our potential parents and ancestors as well, before we were created, maybe we'd avoid a lot of grief. If the revelations proved unsatisfactory, we could then checkout other prospective parents and select healthier antecedents instead. Crazy thought, eh? Yet very appealing. Nevertheless, we are who we are, and have to make the best of it. Indeed, I expect my health problems will likely replicate those from whom I came. I will resemble them in many ways . . . some good and some bad.

Yet, one's birthright isn't as straightforward and immutable as that. Instead, each of us are new creations, whose genetic programming is bound to be different in untold ways. Our uniqueness is governed by the autonomous, amazing, phenomenon of DNA mutations (a spontaneous change in genetic material, the cause of which seems vague). These mutations are presumably initiated during that magical moment of conception. I gather it's a process that occurs in all living organisms during reproduction of the species. But I must beware of undue optimism, for the mutations aren't necessarily improvements. Mutations are like wild cards—capricious, random, and unpredictable. So expect life's unfolding unknowns to lend a wistful character to the future, as well as raising exciting possibilities.

* * *

Lou confidently expected that the surgical removal of the cancerous prostate would lead to a cure with total elimination of cancer, but regrettably it was not to be. He shared that unrealistic hope with most other cancer patients. They terribly wanted to believe that the surgery was all they needed, and were consequently dismayed when it wasn't. Unfair as it seemed, with their lives in a balance, lacking any viable alternative, they chose to forge ahead. The doctor's and hospital's tenacious grips would of necessity continue, involving patients in unsettling and anxiety-filled unknowns. Rarely is surgery alone enough.

Sadly, the bleak postsurgical recurrence of cancer is all too frequent. It seems that no matter how expert the surgeon and how radical the excision of the lesion—including tissue removal from healthy-looking marginal areas—some dispersed and microscopic pernicious cancer cells often remain, and will re-grow. Their threat is multifaceted: cancer cells have incredibly robust growth with incessant division; they are seemingly immortal; malignancies can destroy healthy tissues; and when left untreated, the nutritional demands of these deranged cells subvert the body's normal functions by exploiting an outsized drain on nutritional supplies. Apparently it takes only a minimum number of residual cancer cells to create a menacing recurrence. The ravenous parasitic-like growth of cancer cells eventually undermines the organism's ability to function, and leads to death. The end is characterized by what is known as 'cachexia'—a slow wasting of the body with severe weight loss.

Complications increase when specific cancers have a high tendency to metastasize—that's spreading beyond its site of origin, handily via the blood and lymphatic systems. Hence, remote locations are seeded with cancer cells and new threatening lesions are spawned. Therefore, the routine management for many cancers now calls for postsurgical radiation treatment, chemotherapy alone, or combinations of both, in an attempt to destroy all of the remaining cancer cells.

During Lou's postsurgical recovery, he was informed that radiation of the area should be scheduled. His outward manner didn't reveal how upset he was. The rationale for the radiation treatment was based on the finding during the histo-pathological study of the extirpated prostate: a significant perforation in the gland's capsule existed. Accordingly, cancer cells could have easily—most likely did—spread out into the connective tissue bed from which the prostate was removed. To be safe, radiation of this area was strongly recommended to ensure that any remaining cancer cells were killed, and freedom from the grim malignancy could be more justifiably declared.

* * *

Lou reexamined his critical choice, *The plan to submit to radiation came as a shock. From the moment of the diagnosis through the surgery I'd been eager to proceed, and gratefully followed the Doctor's lead. This time I hesitated, and I believe with good reason. Though my thinking was under-standably somewhat clouded during those early post-op days, when I was barely re-covering from the trauma of the surgery, experiencing complex emotional swings, and with a urinary catheter in place, it never the less made sense to me to reject the radiation . . . at least for the time being.*

I was certainly in favor of killing off any lingering cancer cells with radiation, only I worried that radiation could also damage the delicate surgically repaired tissues. My foremost concern was possible radiation damage to the meticulously reconnected urethra—the canal from the bladder through which urine is discharged. The removal of the prostate, positioned right against the bladder, included that section of the urethra which the walnut-sized gland surrounded.

Even after I was told how the location of the suspected residual malignant site would be precisely determined, to allow for targeted accuracy of the radiation, I still refused treatment. It worried me that the close-by urethra-bladder-interface might also be irradiated (maybe impossible to avoid). This area was freshly repaired and still healing. If the urethral-bladder's surgically reconstructed watertight seal was damaged it could adversely affect my urinary control.... Permanently. It was a risk I feared to take.

Further, the non-selectivity of radiation was an important factor that reinforced my decision —the rays indiscriminately kill cancer cells along with normal cells that happen to be in the vicinity.

But with hindsight, I now understand that to have delayed radiation created a much greater risk. If the cancer cells in the prostate bed had grown vigorously and disseminated widely, then treatment to eradicate the widespread tumors would be unavailable. By the time I agreed to radiation, fortunately that had not occurred. I lucked-out to have cancer cells that — atypically — were slow-growing and sluggish. They remained in situ, and the radiation succeeded in eliminating them.

* * *

For about five years post-op Lou did well. His urinary function was normal, and the annual PSA (prostate specific antigen) blood tests, which monitored prostate cancer cell levels, were basically undetectable (no cancer recurrence). But eventually, those sleepy malicious cancer cells started to re-grow, and his PSA test number began to rise. The test was repeated after only a few months, with the same distressing result. It couldn't be ignored. Prostate cancer was reasserting itself. The Doctor summarized, "Considering the lengthy lag-time since surgery, those cancer cells in the prostate bed seem to have been remarkably slow growing. So it's a safe bet they hadn't metastasized. Lou, go for the radiation, before those little bastards change their mind."

Without hesitation or uncertainty Lou agreed to radiation, though experiencing a measure of rueful apprehension. The treatment included thirty-five very brief radiation exposures (the standard protocol) from which he experienced no side or after-effects. The PSA cooperatively resumed its undetectable reading. Lou was greatly relieved and hoped the reading would stay at zero for the foreseeable future. The PSA blood test would provide the annual reassurance that all was well.

* * *

Lou's inner reflections, *There's nothing quite so awful as to be told your cancer has returned. It's a severe blow. An unwelcome déjà vu. I was incred-ulous, and fervently believed (more likely a futile hope) that somehow a mistake had occurred. Unfortunately the recurrence was validated. All the old fears and anxieties that took me so long to overcome and were buried and forgotten, suddenly reawakened.*

Emotionally I was turned around. It was as though the healthy intervening years had never happened.

All the memories from those worrisome post-op months came flooding back. During those days, stretching to months, I had agonized that my post-op incontinence and impotence would eventually fade—as I was reassured by the doctor—and not become permanent. Now, facing a recurrence, those fears came crashing back, with a vengeance.

In the course of time, I had gratefully, and with considerable relief, totally recovered from both of those ugly post-op liabilities. As I faced radiation, I braced myself for the worst possible aftereffects: that my urinary control, and even my sexual capacity would be adversely effected.

When I restrainedly raised these concerns with the radiologist, he dismissed them out-of-hand and said, "Lou, forget about it. Let me assure you that the radiation will not—the emphasis is on not or never—cause even a brief interference with either your urinary control or your ability to raise as substantial an erection as you're accustomed to. Believe me, we've targeted that one cancer spot with precision. Furthermore, the minimum dosage we apply with each treatment has been adjusted to prevent any side effects, yet is able to kill off those lousy, no-good cells."

He was right. The treatments were uneventful. Also, each radiation exposure was extremely brief. Actually it took me much longer to change out of my street clothes and don a flimsy hospital gown, than it was to be irradiated. And of course, my main fears never materialized: my peeing control was completely unaffected, and I participated in sex, surprisingly, with renewed fervor and vigor.

CHAPTER THIRTEEN

It was a dreary day on the Hudson River. The sky was blanketed with low-hanging dense, grey, stratus-type clouds, which entirely blocked the sun's warm, comforting rays, along with a noticeable drop in temperature. A steady, moist mist hung in the air, with an occasional light drizzle. The unpleasantness of the weather was increased by its penetrating chilly dampness. Visibility was also drastically reduced. From Lou's marina on the East side of the River, the town of Nyack—only two-and-a-half-miles directly across on the Hudson's West side—usually clearly seen was now barely visible. The boating season was coming to an end. Moreover, the drop in temperature signaled a necessary clothing change: from the scant summer attire of shorts, t-shirts, and bare feet; folks now dressed in long pants, sweaters, wind and water repellent jackets, and their boating shoes were worn with socks.

The abrupt weather change with cooler temperatures and increased precipitation were harbingers of Autumn's arrival. Among the folks at the marina the meteorological opinion that the seasons changed more rapidly on the River, was a near-sacrosanct truth. No one posed arguments to the contrary. Its validity appeared self-evident to everyone.

The Hudson Valley's lush surrounding hills of verdant beauty — amazingly still redolent of its early primitive grandeur — provided unlimited boating opportunities throughout most of the River's drainage, yet afforded only a limited season. This was to be expected due to the River's geographic location within Northern latitudes, extending its upper reaches far north into New York State. Thus, boating lasted only four-months, at best.

Early on in Spring there's a manic-like rush to get boats back into the water; and then the calendar quickly winds down and the boating season draws to a close. It's time to haul them out again. It's a frenzied cycle—highlighted with brief, wonderfully fulfilling and absorbing cruising interludes.

To those afflicted with the passion—referred to by the aficionados as 'boating mania'—it's somehow all worthwhile. Though the time available for boating is limited, the ambience has an unusually strong appeal. It's a world set apart from one's common orderly life, with different rules and challenges, where one can be refreshed and recharged.

Winter comes rushing in after a typically brief Autumn. It's a natural cyclical event, whose sudden frosty temperatures are low enough to freeze the inshore waters and seriously threaten sleek fiberglass-hulled boats still tied-up in the River. These popular modern hulls are vulnerable to be crushed by ice. It begins with the freezing of water: As the water changes from liquid into ice its bulk expands. Therefore, as ice accumulates around a boat with persistent, continuous pressure created by the ice buildup against the vessel's relatively brittle fiberglass shell, a calamitous hull collapse can occur.

Such severe damage could lead to the likely scrapping of the boat. Thus, at this time of year on the Hudson, the owners of fiber-glass boats actively make plans for the timely removal of their vessels from the water and secure storage on land. It's a hectic time for them, which involves some labor intensive effort (much by the owners) and incurs considerable cost.

Strangely, there are always a few hardy folks who are determined to live on their boats all year round. To protect their hulls from the ice they employ an air-bubbling device that is floated around and close to the boat. The continuous agitation of the water by the bubbling air effectively prevents ice formation in the vicinity. All goes well as long as the electrical power continues to reliably flow. Prudent skippers also provide for back-up battery power to automatically takeover if the electricity failed, or alternatively prefer to run the device entirely on batteries. The whole process seems risky, especially when temperatures drop dreadfully low, producing massive ice floes that drift unpredictably.

And of course, keeping warm and living in a very confined space, are conditions that apparently appeals only to a select few.

* * *

One day during Lou's post-op recovery, he insisted to Nicole that he was strong enough to drive to the marina for the day. The cancer business, which Lou referred to as a "diversion from real life," had unmercifully cutout the heart of the boating season, and left him only its tail end. Impatiently, he couldn't wait to get back to the marina to check on the boat. On this occasion he went alone. Nicole was glad to see him feeling better, and chose not to go along on such a nasty day. After all she thought, *He's not going sailing, only fussing around to get the boat ready to be put away. If it were up to me, I'd still get rid of it for good, within a heartbeat.*

* * *

In addition, it was time to make arrangements for the dry-docking (hauling the boat out, critically winterizing the engines, and draining water out of all lines with antifreeze replacement). Storage under cover on land at Peterson's across the river was planned, with the boat brought into one of their large sheds, or, if kept outdoors, it would be wrapped and sealed tight in plastic.

Lou wasn't surprised to find the marina quiet, and as far as he could tell no one else was around. He also noted that a surprising number of boats had already been removed for winter storage. Some of the long-standing members who enjoyed special privileges, had taken advantage of their option to store their boats on the marina's adjacent large parking lot. They claimed it saved them a substantial amount of money. The savings were only realized if the owners undertook all the winterizing preparations themselves, in particular, fastening the boat cover securely enough to reliably protect the vessel from the ravages of weather during the many month's hiatus before the next season. In addition to the time-consuming hard work involved, they had better perform all that was required with the necessary know-how and skill, or they might put the boat in jeopardy.

None of that appealed to Lou. He enjoyed running the boat, and employed others to care for the grit and grime of its maintenance.

* * *

Lou was startled by the sound of the cabin door opening. At first he thought, *Maybe I hadn't closed it tightly, or could the wind have blown it open*? When he turned from his seat at the dining table, where he was sipping a mug of hot tea while reviewing his collection of operational manuals (the indispensable sources of maintenance data for each and every device on the boat), to his amazement there stood Jane in the doorway. He quickly rose, faced her directly, felt confused as though waking from deep sleep, and was speechless. Jane broke the silence, "Hi, old buddy. Remember me? As a happy surprise, I'm the one who likes to show up unexpectedly. At least that's how it worked out last time. Aren't you going to invite me in?"

The sound of her voice cleared his bewilderment. A wide smile of unambiguous pleasure lit up his face. He was delighted to see her, and answered, "Dear, Jane, must you ask?" They stood looking at each other for an extended moment before Lou resumed, "I might not have expected you, but seeing you again after so long, especially on the boat, is unbelievable. You are a dream come true. Sitting alone in the boat, all I could think about was how much I wished you were here with me, and incredibly here you are."

Jane's face brightened. A delicate glow had spread across her pale, rain-dampened cheeks. Her immediate heartfelt reply, barely above a whisper was, "What a lovely flattering thing to say to a gal. I'm pleased you haven't lost the touch."

Then in rapid fire she started talking, "I worried the Doc's might have completely done you in. Welcome back. When you hadn't gotten in touch with me for longer than expected, I started to wonder that once you had me you were no longer interested."

Lou continued to be struck with Jane's forthright ease in not only talking about sex, but also her lusty, uninhibited participation, the recollections of which profoundly titillated him. The unfavorable contrast with Nicole's silent coyness came to mind.

"Fortunately Nicole and I are good friends," continued Jane. "We regularly talk on the phone. I know you asked her not to speak about your prostate problem. You wanted it kept as a private matter. But like all women, she needed someone to share her fears with, and to tell of the difficult time you both were going through. I listened sympathetically, of course, and was terribly upset and appalled for your sake. I felt awful when I learned the details of the hospitalization and surgery. But honestly, I was also selfishly relieved that I finally understood why you had neglected me."

She had entered the cabin while talking, removed her wet hooded jacket, and hung it on the coat hook on the closed door. With an expression of resignation and annoyance she tried to finger-push her hair into a semblance of order. After fluffing-out her rich, long, blond locks, she added, "Nothing like a hood and wet weather to ruin one's crowning glory. I probably look like something the cat dragged in." Her captivating smile made Lou's heart beat faster.

"Jane, you look absolutely ravishing. Why are we standing and gabbing away like strangers. So please sit down. I bet a mug of hot tea would be in order to clear the chill."

She took a seat on the sleeping sofa near the door and answered, "The tea sounds just right, but only if you'll come and join me on the couch."

They made no attempt to sit apart. Soon their mugs were put aside. As Lou inhaled, Jane's enchanting, subtle, and delicate scent he felt stirrings he hadn't experienced in a long time, and tantalizing images of their prior sexual encounter came to mind.

Yet, Lou hesitated, trying hard not to seem too impulsive.

Their legs gently brushed and while talking their shoulders made contact. Finally when the superficial conversation lagged, he could contain himself no longer. He reached for her, placed his arm around her waist and, as she readily yielded, he slowly pulled her to him. With his left hand he gently turned her face and they eagerly kissed. The embrace was with abandon, needy and hungry. They grasped each other firmly with passion. and held tight. It was obvious their separation had been too long. They relished holding each other, delighted in the physical contact, and were loath to let go.

With a deep sigh of regret, Lou abruptly broke contact and sat back. Jane, flushed and a little breathless, promptly said, “Lou my love, you hold back. Was I wrong coming to the boat? Or maybe it’s all over with us?” With a nervous, unconscious gesture she pushed strands of loose hair back away from her face, sat upright, and added, “Please tell me straight-out how we stand. I’m a big girl and can deal with the truth.”

Lou warmly smiled and responded, “Fear not, Jane. Though the truth is abundantly joyful, it is also a bit complicated. First and most important is my deep love for you, and how I yearn and want you more than ever. Please never doubt it. Secondly, it seems my recovery is not yet complete. In addition to the slow healing of the extensive incision through my abdominal muscles which still sends pain signals when I overexert myself, there is also the curious issue—and here he paused and smiled—of my inability to raise an adequate erection. The Doc's assured me it will fully recover in time. I’m happy to report that it’s beginning to happen, but not quite all there yet.” He stopped at this point, chuckled quietly while watching her and asked, “Am I being too candidly clinical for you?”

Jane smiled with a glint in her eyes, took his hands and raised them to her mouth for a kiss, and said, "Not at all. I'm not squeamish in the least, and am prepared to handle life's distasteful offerings which inevitably will involve all of us, one way or another. Actually, I'm delighted to find you more robust than I anticipated." Still holding his hands tightly, with steady eye contact, and in characteristic calm and confident manner, she added, "And you shouldn't ever doubt that I'm eager for your love. I'll be patient. When the time comes and you want me, I'll be there. You'll always find me a willing, loving partner."

Caught without warning, Lou suddenly experienced an unsettling wave of conflicting emotions. In his depleted physical and mental state, he was unprepared for the disruption. It was a poignant mix of intense feelings: On the one hand, he was overcome with happiness at Jane's outpouring of love, which he genuinely reciprocated; yet on the other hand, he also had deep concern that all of his negative, bottled up feelings about the surgery were now unraveling. During those long stressful months he had suppressed his fears, and kept them to himself. On the surface he had always maintained a cheerful and optimistic bearing with considerable determination. He feared that anything less could lead to a breakdown of his defenses, and loss of his ability to sustain a positive outlook. Moreover, Nicole was having a hard time dealing with the serious nature of his illness, and depended on his strength and repeated assurances that all would be well.

Jane's impetuous arrival changed everything. While sitting alone on the boat, in an empty marina, on a bleak, depressingly rainy day, he had been feeling sorry for himself, and was drained of energy or purpose. Her decision to seek him out, and then her bold expressions of love were unexpected gifts, which revitalized him with newfound strength and optimism. He was thrilled and felt undyingly grateful. But his veneer of self-containment weakened. At that critical moment, he was struck with an awareness, *How very much I do love Jane, above all else, and hope to share the rest of my life with her. All other issues no longer matter. With the past about to be wiped clean, and a positive future imagined, I feel elated and reborn.*

Those supercharged emotions taxed his composure. The pressure built, and he had become aware of a strange, extraordinary sense of vulnerability and weakness. As the reaction took hold of him, he feared he might embarrass himself and cry. It was all too much. Despairing that he was about to breakdown, Lou pulled Jane to him, buried his face on her bosom and smothered the sobs that broke free.

Jane's tears also flowed, and with Lou held firmly in her arms she stroked his hair, patted his back, and encouragingly murmured, "That's O.K., my love. Let it all out. It's way past time you did. The worst is over, dearest, and you'll be better than ever. What a glorious day to have found each other once again. The bloody rain is the perfect backdrop. The heavens are joining us as we cry with hope that we'll wash away our pain and rejoice another day. Darling Lou, we are bonded forever in love and need. Though today you need my shoulder, tomorrow I'll probably need yours. Feel happy, the best of times are just ahead."

It took a while for them to calm down. Lou sat back, looked lovingly at Jane, and before he could say anything Jane put a finger against his lips, bent forward, kissed him gently, and added, "Hush now. Rest quietly for a while. Enough said."

* * *

Before long they stirred and Jane asked, "Well, skipper, it's time we got down to work. What has to be done?"

With both of them working together, they soon had almost everything cleaned up. All foodstuffs were removed and placed in a large heavy-duty garbage bag that Lou had brought, and it would be discarded in the marina's dumpster as they left. Extra linens, blankets, and Nicole's and Lou's assorted clothing items were folded and stacked in a duffle bag for removal. Books, manuals, navigational charts with plotting instruments, log book, boxes of tools, and several containers of various parts were all stored in lockable-cabinets. The cleaning supplies were all checked to identify those ready for discard: empty and near-empty containers; used rags; along with anything worn enough to merit replacement. The useful items were left on board.

All that remained were the linens in the V-birth. Lou had sat down on the couch and appeared a bit tired. Jane walked over to him, bent down, kissed him, and while holding his chin in her hands said, “Lou, now that we have everything organized, how about a lie-down in the V-birth for a rest and a comforting cuddle before we strip the bed?” Lou looked up, smiled, and answered, “I don’t know about the rest bit, but the comforting sounds irresistibly appealing. I welcome all I can get. Your thought to use the V-birth is a great idea. It’ll be a fitting farewell to it and the boat for a while."

Without another word, they removed their outer warm clothing, and with only a minimum of undergarments remaining they crawled into the V-birth and under the blankets. Without delay they reached for each other, hugged voraciously and both laughed spontaneously. Lou was the first to speak, “Of course all this body contact is simply for the purpose of sharing the warmth on a cold day.” They laughed again. As they held each other tightly in a full-body embrace, some inevitable squirming and body-rubbing took place. Jane soon sighed, unhooked her brassier and slipped it off while squirming out of her panties. Lou then dropped his shorts. Jane pulled his head onto her breasts, lifted one leg over him and pressed firmly. Her murmurs of delight were unexpectedly interrupted.

She pushed Lou back, looked down, and exclaimed with surprise and excitement, "My, my, see who has joined us." Lou knew she was referring to his fully raised and firm erection.

Before he could say anything or move, Jane said, "Lou, my love, now you just stay where you are, turn onto your back and be still. I'll mount you. Let me do the work. This way we'll avoid any strain on that lovely but sensitive belly of yours. And unequivocally your full recovery will be appropriately received with complete satisfaction.

Their celebratory sexual coupling was unanticipated, and brought Lou a satisfying physical release with immense pleasure, and alleviated a painful emotional issue. He had worried that maybe that critical part of life was over. The last of his lingering fears were effectively relieved. He knew he was fully restored once again as a whole man, and rejoiced silently, but profoundly. He laid back, cradled in Jane's arms, and allowed himself to drift off into a peaceful sleep . . . ostensibly for the first time in a long time.

CHAPTER FOURTEEN

The ensuing months turned out to be more trying than anticipated. Jane and Lou continued to meet as often as possible, in one clandestine fashion after another. But, always seeking a furtive encounter began to cause a strain. With a strengthened relationship, they increasingly despaired over the unavoidable lengthy separations, and felt their meetings had developed an unpleasant sordid tone, which they resented. In time, they jointly came to recognize that a change had to be made. They would be circumspect, but a more open, honest arrangement was needed. Finally they agreed that divorces were the inescapable solutions. As soon as feasible, they intended to follow with their own marriage.

Though they shared a dread of the imponderable legal complexities and emotional turmoil involved, they were determined to proceed with the divorces.

And yet, with the passage of time, circumstances had so irrevocably altered that they reluctantly decided to cancel the impending divorce plans—at least for the time being. Quite unexpectedly, Jane's husband Oscar had recently been diagnosed with type-1 *Diabetes Mellitus*. Unfortunately, he had disregarded the growing intensity of inconvenient and unpleasant symptoms, and when finally had sought medical help (after much hesitation) his condition was advanced. The diagnosis was not obscure. As he was examined, Oscar's description of his complaints reinforced the doctor's early clinical impression: Oscar undoubtedly had *Diabetes*. With doleful resignation, the doctor thought to himself, *Here's another unnecessarily sick, impotent, obese, middle-aged male, with an acknowledged sedentary life style, and whose unpleasant breath typically smells sour, with a sweet-metalic mix. It all adds up to a serious Diabetic condition. I am certain the blood tests will invariably confirm the diagnosis. And what's so frustrating is that in Oscar's case the Diabetes was preventable; if he hadn't excessively violated all the well-known rules for sustaining good health, he'd likely be OK today. All his education and intelligence didn't help. I'll do what I can, but unless he gets a grip on his diet and incorporates some exercise, I suspect the prognosis will not be favorable.*

Oscar became an insulin-dependent patient. However as foreseen, the doctor's efforts to establish a normal, stable, blood sugar level failed. A major contributing factor to this difficulty was Oscar's inability to consistently comply with the specifically prescribed diet. This undermined his treatment and led to continuing illness. Therefore, his weight reduction was negligible, if any at all, and he remained grossly overweight. Jane intuitively suspected that he cheated by bringing many of the prohibited foods to his office. Despite all efforts by his doctor along with Jane's repeated urgings, he made little progress in helping to control the disease. Eventually, Oscar's large toe on his left foot had to be amputated after it turned hopelessly black. *Diabetics* with uncontrollable blood sugar were especially vulnerable to necrosis of the blood vessels supplying the toes.

This *Diabetic* complication can be very problematic, leading to periodic episodes, often ascending the leg, and requiring repeated surgeries.

Sadly, it became abundantly clear that Oscar wasn't sufficiently cooperative or even motivated to follow the basic medical advice. In increasing ways he became more invalided and often turned to Jane for moral and physical support. Though Jane suspected that Oscar's unwillingness or inability to help himself was possibly a manifestation of some deep-seated neurosis, she quietly accepted responsibility to look after him, and remained married. When she explained to Lou why her decision to seek a divorce would have to be shelved for the present, they reached for each other and hugged, as she hid her tear-stained face on his shoulder. It was evident to

Lou that Jane's decision to care for Oscar would be a stressful burden. Her strong sense of obligation prevented anything less. In addition, the disruption in their divorce plans were an additional cause for her distress and frustration. Lou loved and admired her even more for her principled choice, but also felt bitterly disappointed.

Seen as inevitable, Lou's relationship with Nicole had been adversely effected. They didn't talk about it, but they knew a change had occurred. For her part, Nicole had plans of her own. She was determined to avoid her participation in boating as much as possible. If it came down to it, she would be satisfied never to go to the marina again. Moreover, she made arrangements to resume her career as a real-estate sales agent. With her license still current, her previous employer was glad to have her back. The work schedule was always flexible enough to fit her availability and accommodate other commitments.

* * *

By the time the next boating season arrived they all—collectively and separately—had entered a new phase in their lives. Divorce plans were of necessity on hold. The cancellation was disappointing to Jane and Lou, while paradoxically they also were spared considerable anxiety. They became more relaxed with their ongoing relationship, and openly moved on with plans for the future. Their determined focus on the positive prospects of their shared lives helped them remain upbeat and happy. With the new boating season at hand, they began to plot a number of exciting extended-range cruises. Doubtlessly their compatible enthusiasm for boating was a strong bond, and they forged ahead with passion and animation. They also soon surmounted and put aside any remnants of nagging emotional hang-ups—about their marital failures—which freed them of any sense of remorse or guilt.

Oscar at least minimally complied with the need to administer his thrice daily insulin injections, but otherwise didn't make any effort to change his self-destructive life style. He had long ago lost all interest in sex, and seemed unconcerned about Jane's relationship with Lou. Just as long as Jane was reasonably available for help if needed, he was satisfied.

Nicole had announced she was finished with boating, and increasingly would be busy with work. Since they never openly faced up to the change in their lives, her reaction to Lou's current involvement with Jane wasn't discussed. Without fanfare, one day Nicole moved out of their bedroom and settled into one of the other rooms. To their mutual satisfaction, the move was timely and prudent. It eliminated the last vestige of potential for strained intimate contacts. As usual they continued to share the household chores along with its fiscal management, remained cordial, and lived separate lives.

It wasn't surprising that Nicole and Jane's friendship had abruptly ended, with a cessation of all contacts, particularly by phone. No angry, hysterical confrontations were involved. All parties understood what had occurred, quietly accepted the new realignment with composure—while possibly concealing a measure of relief.

.Nicole felt free to pursue a career, and was open to new relationships. Her sense of relief from any involvement with boating led to a refreshing mood improvement: her long-suppressed tensions about boating were washed away. She became optimistic and more lighthearted than she had been for quite a while.

Oscar ignored his inner struggles and conflicts about his health, and was comforted that he didn't have to concern himself any longer with Jane's sexual needs, which always had overwhelmed him.

Decidedly, Jane and Lou were heavily intoxicated with each other, and could hardly believe in their good fortune to have found such a glorious and unexpected second chance at love and life.

* * *

They had picked a beautiful sunny day, with little or no wind, for their first cruise out to

Long Island Sound. Jane was bubbling with enthusiasm, and her contagious high spirits thrilled Lou. She stood next to him on the bridge, with her right arm firmly wrapped around his waist, and the navigational charts clutched tightly in her left. Jane laughed and said, "Lou, what you didn't know about me was my fascination with maps of all kinds. It started with the common road map. Next I became interested in global geographical depiction's, and began to collect world maps, including a few nifty globes. I have an incredible collection."

"You're more and more amazing," said Lou. "Collecting maps is surely engaging, though I suspect somewhat unusual. Would it be possible to be bring some to the boat? As it happens, maps have also always appealed to me, and I would love to see them." Lou grinned widely and added, "Now I know an additional reason to be turned on by you . . . of course, talking about being turned on, if the truth be told, I must admit how hopelessly enslaved I am by your provocative pheromones."

"Good!" replied Jane with gusto, as they laughed. "Sure, I'll be delighted to gather them up. I think one medium-sized cardboard box ought to hold an interesting mix. It'll be fun studying maps together. But now that you brought up the subject of sex, I believe I also have uncovered an unexpected new aphrodisiac," answered Jane with a sham serious expression. "I'll choose an enticing map of some exotic country from my collection, open it out for you to absorb, and when you're properly aroused, I'll have you."

They laughed again, kissed, and Lou said, "No need to go to such trouble. You know, my dear, I'm real easy. The surgery didn't slow me down one bit. All it takes is a come-hither look from you and I'm ready."

"Say, lover, all this talk is going to distract us from the cruising," said Jane. "Better save it for later. Now I want you to know that I've studied the navigational charts for this trip and am eager to show off. How about it, skipper, can I consider myself the ship's Navigator? The official title would really suit me well. What ya say, eh?"

"I have no doubt that you're going to be a superb Navigator. As far as I can see, you're a natural born sailor, and before long, you'll be able to run this boat by yourself. So, as part of your continuing training, I've planned to upgrade your handling of the helm. We'll start you off as we approach the waters of the Sound. Naturally, keep in mind, that as the Skipper of this craft I enjoy all traditional rights and privileges, especially those of cohabitation with the lesser crew."

"I would have it no other way, Sir," answered Jane while saluting Lou, "and eagerly look forward to your exercise of that right."

Their continuous, unrestrained sexual banter never let up. It was a form of playfulness in which they felt relaxed and relished the titillating humor. Like a breath of fresh air that cooled the feverish, a marked interpersonal sexual change had dramatically swept widely through society in recent years. The private sexual lives of many were favorably effected and improved.

For countless folks, sexual encounters had been awkwardly more ritualistic than passionate (encumbered with a measure of guilt by some) while confined to a bed in a darkened room. The changes swept away restrictive attitudes and tight inhibitions, and replaced them with an healthy, open, celebratory recognition that the need for love and sex were universal human attributes. Explicitly, the drive for carnal pleasure was viewed as normal, equally experienced by both men and women.

Lou and Jane didn't invent this change, but gloried in how it enriched their relationship.

When they passed under the majestic Throggs Neck Suspension Bridge, Jane knowingly said, "Skipper, there's City Island off our port. We must plan to tie-up there before long, and pig-out on some steamers and lobsters at one of their famous seafood eateries. Something to look forward to."

"Just hearing you talk about the food, makes my mouth water," replied Lou. "Don't worry about it. When we get to Greenwich, you'll be pleased with the seafood at the convenient dockside restaurant. It'll be a leisurely meal, since we departed early enough to allow plenty of time to cruise back after lunch."

Coming up straight ahead was the incongruous looking *Stepping Stones Light House*, towards which Lou had intentionally steered on a collision course, while looking calm and noncommittal.

Picking up on his charade-like unconcerned pose, Jane sounded similarly nonplussed when she quietly announced, "By the way, Skipper, if I may infringe on your meditation, unless you intend to 'Kamikaze-like' kill us all, you had better alter course to the port to avoid crashing into *Stepping Stones*. Also, by all means avoid the seemingly clear water on the *Light House's* other side, unless you'd prefer ripping the bottom out of our boat."

"Right-on, chief Navigator, I got your message," said Lou with a broad smile. "You've earned your rating today, and an extra dessert at lunch. Now, Jane, slip over and take the wheel, and steer us as you advised. Just make the port turn slow and easy. Ignore the throttles for the time being. Keep *Stepping Stones* reasonably close on our starboard, so as to leave room for incoming traffic on our port. As you might have surmised, boating has rules of the road, as there are for automobiles. The most basic and useful is to pass oncoming boats on your port side. Imagine the chaos without such a rule."

Jane was thrilled to be at the helm, and followed Lou's instructions in a confident manner, as if she had been at the controls for years. Smoothly the boat was guided around *Stepping Stones* and well-out into the middle of the Sound. Lou noted with a smile how Jane's concentration with the conning of the boat had momentarily quieted her down, at least for the time being. Her attention was completely riveted on what was out in front, while listening attentively for Lou's guidance.

"Most of the time," continued Lou, "while cruising along, both throttles are kept at the same R.P.M.s. When you want to slow down or speed up, both throttles must be adjusted equally, as long as you intend to continue going straight ahead. Notice that both throttles are now at the same forward location, with identical R.P.M.s registering on the gauges. It took me quite a while to learn how to tune the engines so as to precisely balance them. I never could have done it on my own. I'm in debt to one of the expert mechanic guys in the marina, who taught me not only how to tune engines but also tipped me off about the special tools. I knew how to drive a car from before my tenth birthday, but frankly never looked under the hood. So, it was about time I learned something about gasoline engine maintenance. The downside of mechanic's work is how awfully greasy and dirty one gets." Lou paused, shook his head and added, "Nonetheless, I enjoy it and don't hesitate to admit how satisfied I am with my new skills."

"And I'm proud as hell of you, Lou," called out Jane. "Another dimension has been added. And who knows, maybe someday you'll even teach me how to do it. What a blast we're having. Oops, I better not get distracted while running this ship. Lou, I'm starting to relax at the helm, and there sure is something exhilarating about being up here on the bridge with the wheel in my hands. It's not quite orgiastic, but someplace not too far behind. Feeling in control of this huge boat is mind-boggling. What's most amazing is that I have an uncanny sense of personal power which is almost palpable. Wow!"

"And it's just the beginning for you," commented Lou. "No doubt running a boat is an incredible turn-on. I must add, and not for the first time, how absolutely thrilled I am with you. Is it possible that you are my doppel-ganger? That is my ghostly double."

Jane laughed out loud, and said, "What-ever you say, Lou. If you're right, I hope our compatibility lasts indefinitely and grows ever sweeter with time." She paused, and looked lovingly over her shoulder "Now I'm going to impress you with how well I did my navigation homework, so listen up. Once past the *Light*

House, the Sound spreads out rapidly with increasing width. The widest point is some 20-miles across, located approximately at the middle of the 90-mile-long, essentially East-West Sound. This offers boaters a vast deep water basin in which to enjoy boating, with land always in sight. Almost impossible to get lost. Many consider it the best recreational boating area in the country."

"We're getting close to Greenwich, Jane, so it's a good time to tell you about the aids to navigation that will guide us," Lou said, after he took control of the helm. "Not only do they point the way, but also take us through a safe passage. Without them, sailing safely into these inshore waters and narrow channels, would be almost impossible. Could you imagine those dangerous old days before navigational aids, and even further back before the waters were charted for depths and underwater obstacles."

"My god," exclaimed Jane, "ships must have had a terrible time. Running aground was likely a common risk, and wreckage's with loss of life a frequent horrible outcome."

"You're absolutely right. We owe a debt of gratitude to those early mariners who were the first to boldly sail these waters and bequeath to us their hard-learned findings."

They were just entering into the fairly lengthy approach into Greenwich when Lou resumed, "For our purposes there are two types of Aids to Navigation: the Red ones have even numbers, which increase as you proceed inland; and the Green ones have odd numbers. Just remember the old saying, 'Red-Right-Returning' and the opposite when leaving. That means to pass the Red *Buoys* on the right side (starboard) of the vessel when entering a port, or a river, as we will soon."

"I've locked onto that rule and won't forget it," replied Jane. "So that's what all those floating objects are for, and I imagine there's also a system to their shapes."

"Good for you, love," said Lou, delighted with her involvement. "The U.S. Coast Guard, who established and maintains the Aids, thought of everything. When visibility is poor, such as at night, heavy fog and rain, or any condition that makes it difficult or impossible to distinguish the colors and numbers of the Aids, then their differing shapes help. The unlighted Red *Buoys* are shaped like an inverted cone, and are called *Nuns.* The Green ones are flat-topped cylinders, and simply called *Cans.* Today more and more of all *Buoys* are equipped with radar reflectors, to allow them to show up on radar scopes when visibility deteriorates. The limiting caveat is that the radar images can't tell one shape from another. We don't have radar, so my knowledge is only hearsay. I gather once the *Buoy* is located on radar, then a ship's spotlight is used to identify it. Those who have radar swear by it, and claim they wouldn't sail without it. Frankly, I'm not interested in boating at night, and try my best to avoid bad weather. As far as I'm concerned, boating is supped to be fun, so let's focus on clear sailing, good food and drink, and concentrate on soul-satisfying sex whenever the mood strikes us."

"Amen," replied Jane quickly, smiling with obvious enthusiasm, coupled with a tight hug and kiss.

CHAPTER FIFTEEN

"Now I want our lovely Navigator to pay strict attention to the next lesson in Aids to Navigation. It's not sexy but very important. As we approach the turn into Greenwich, which is right across the border into Connecticut, I'll be slowing down. We're looking for the Red *Buoy* number "1" which will mark the entrance to the channel into Greenwich," explained Lou. "Like all these larger, open framed *Buoys*, it has a continuously flashing light on top and gives out a characteristic sound. Jane, kindly look at the chart, find the symbol for *Buoy* number "1" and tell me what you see."

"Yes sir, Skipper," eagerly said Jane, "just give me a moment to locate it. Ah, here it is, and it says 'gong.' Do all these big *Buoys* have gongs?"

"No, some have bells," answered Lou. "These lights and sounds were an invaluable help in locating the *Buoys* during darkness and conditions of restricted visibility. And the same lateral system rule applies to all Aids: we pass these lighted Red *Buoys* on our starboard side. Also like the smaller *Cans* and *Nuns* the large *Buoy's* numbers will increase as we enter, with even numbers on Red ones and odd on the Green."

"Three cheers for the U.S. Coast Guard." said Jane, "and many thanks for the explanation. Seems confusing at first, but the logic of the system really makes it easy to remember."

* * *

The singular arrangement of their personal lives continued without disruption. Everyone involved settled into the new dynamics of their relationships, with which they, by and by, felt comfortable, as if it had always been this way. Jane continued to live with Oscar and dutifully tended to his increasing health-related needs and dependence.

Lou and Nicole shared their home, and as the tension in their relationship faded a surprisingly unexpected friendship emerged. Nicole eventually found sharing some work experiences and problems with Lou to be satisfying, and he proved to be a good listener with constructive input. All went well as long as conversations were restricted to neutral subjects, and mention of the boat with Lou's relationship with Jane were avoided.

Lou and Jane had a wonderful time. They spent long weekends on the boat, and on occasion extended their stay beyond. It was as though their real life existed only on the boat. Jane liked to characterize this boating season, prefaced with a hug and kiss, by saying, "Lou, my love, this summer on the boat is really like an extended honeymoon. Aren't we an amazing couple." Lou held her tight and responded softly, " Hush now. Just go with the warm flow."

All the many chores were shared. When it came to cooking, it turned out that Lou had a better feel for it and usually was in charge. Yet the demand on his culinary skills weren't too onerous, since they often frequented area restaurants for dinner. Though the exception was breakfast. Jane was an early riser and enjoyed catering to Lou in the morning. Lou relished that special time when he had just awakened after a restful night's sleep. He watched from the V-berth as Jane fussed around, preparing the food and setting the table, while usually clad only in a t-shirt and—at times—panties. If he was inclined to a pietistic faith, which he wasn't, then at these moments he would utter a prayer of gratitude for the wonder of his love for Jane. Deep in his heart he knew that whatever life brought, his love for her was eternal.

They liked to work together, and took pleasure in keeping the boat looking spick-and-span. Routinely after each cruise they never skipped a thorough clean-up drill: to restore the hull's bright shine it was washed to remove remnants of salt residue and other foreign matter from the River; to maintain the stainless steel railing's metallic glow (they learned that stainless meant less stain not none) they were scrubbed with specially treated pads that removed any blemish or tarnish; and all the wooden trim were kept lustrous with an oil-based polish. On dark, gloomy or rainy days, they busied themselves in the cabin. Engine maintenance took much time, especially with Jane's fascination with the process and desire to learn how it's done. After a while, Lou had to admit she could tune the engines quicker and more precisely than he could. Jane surprised herself to discover how mechanically adept and interested she was. Of course, planning new cruises and plotting out waypoints for the Loran were precise technically absorbing projects that appealed to both of them.

Within the constraints of the weather, they spent much of their cruising time out on the Long Island Sound. Greenwich and Stamford, which was a little further east, were destinations that fit into a day trip. When time and inclination permitted, the large marina in Stamford harbor was a favorite for an over-night stay. It was well maintained, had secure entrance gates, floating docks, and a fine adjacent dockside restaurant. They often returned to Greenwich for lunch at its dock-side seafood restaurant, whose atmosphere and food they enjoyed. Conveniently there was a very long dock which could accommodate many boats, and when filled a team of dock boys would double up the overflow—

called rafting. On a busy day it sort of looked like a nautical parking lot.

A big project was afoot. Lou and Jane were involved in planning a lengthy week-long vacation cruise for the latter part of August. Their destination was the Essex Island Marina, which from all reports and readings, was probably the best and most attractive all-around marina on the Sound. It occupied a modest-sized island in the harbor of the charming, Early American Village of Essex.

Their neighbor, Frank, who had sailed the Sound for years and was delighted to share information, was most enthusiastic about the trip to Essex. It didn't take much to get him to provide a detailed description of the Marina, the Village, and its access from the Sound. On a pleasant afternoon, they invited Frank to come aboard for cocktails. Seated in the open aft cockpit with a drink and some crackers with assorted cheeses, Frank happily answered all their questions . . . plus.

"Essex is some three and a half miles up the Connecticut River," began Frank. "Make your turn at the Red bell *Buoy* number "8." The channel access to the River between long rock jetties is relatively narrow, so next look for Red "2" which will guide you through and into the River itself. From here on up to Essex the water is wide and deep. Only concern is that this lower part of the River is patrolled by marine police who are serious about imposing restrictions on speed, and they mean no wake. Speed must be limited to 5-mph to avoid wakes, which is slightly above idle speed. Once you pass under a railroad bridge and then the Connecticut Turnpike Bridge you can increase speed, but don't race and only leave a minimal wake. Essex is on your port side with a well-marked entrance. The approach to the Marina affords a good view of the town. As you come around a gradual bend, the River widens considerably on its western side to reveal the old Town of Essex nestled deeply among gentle hills that reach down to the water's edge. A well-marked channel guides the way to the Marina, set on an island, directly across from the center of town. The 150-foot channel separating the island from the mainland creates a special sense of privacy in the Marina."

Jane asked, "Frank, how do you get from the island to the town? Is there a bridge?"

Frank nodded and answered, "Good question. They thought of everything. There's a constantly-running small ferry to carry people across. I think it runs all night, so folks can return to their boat at any hour, pointedly for those very late ones making it back after an overly-long-lasting party ashore. As you are aware, the protocol when you arrive at a marina is to steer to the Dockmaster's office.

At the Essex Island it's a little shack you can't miss, right there as you enter. Just idle a few yards out, and blow your horn if overlooked. Promptly a young dock boy or girl will cheerfully greet you. With reservations (a must) confirmed, they will give you a slip location with directions. By the way, you must have dinner at the old landmark Griswold Inn, built in 1776. It's a popular place, so when you call the Marina for reservations request that they make a reservation at the Griswold for you. The place fills up early, so if you want a particular time for dinner and not have to wait, don't forget to ask them to arrange it when you call. As a classy extra, you will also be told at check-in that your dinner reservation as requested was confirmed. Well, by the time you locate your slip, and it might take a while due to the Marina's size, there waiting to help tie-up will be the smiling dock boy. It's the only marina I know of that provides that kind of service."

"Frank, I'm really impressed with all this invaluable info," said Jane. "It's like listening to a fascinating lecture. By the way can I refill your drink?"

"Lou, you got yourself a hell of a woman. She knows how to flatter a guy. Thank you, Jane, but one is enough at this time of day. You're going to love the Marina. They have a huge pool, immaculate toilet and shower facilities, and washers and driers if needed. Finally, spend time wandering around the town. You'll enjoy the look and feel of the Colonial ambiance, along with the many tastefully appointed shops, from nautical supplies, to books and clothing, and a selection of restaurants."

"Frank, one more question," asked Lou. "We're thinking of stopping at Mattituck on the way out. Any thoughts or suggestions?"

"Mattituck you say. Haven't thought about it in years. Think I stayed there once. It's interesting that going east along the northern coast of Long Island, after about midway, the only harbor with a marina is Mattituck, and it's way out on the Island's North Fork. You almost don't need a *Buoy* to find the Mattituck Inlet, since sitting a little ways out is what is called a Deep-Draft Offshore Platform. It's where oil tankers tie-up, and pump out the oil, which then flows through pipelines to storage tanks. A pretty impressive setup, that keeps the big tankers out near the ocean where they don't have to sail into the urban waters. I believe much of our fuel for this area is delivered right there. In any event, there is the Green gong *Buoy"3A"* to confirm the Inlet's location. Be prepared for the Mattituck Creek to take a couple of sharp turns at the beginning before it straightens out. A busy fishing fleet works out of the Inlet, and will likely be docked on one side. Big smelly old vessels, but we do like our fish and should be grateful to them. Ignore any watery feeds that flow into the Creek, and follow the main channel straight to the end, where you'll find the marina. It's quite basic, no frills, and not very large, so make a reservation. I do recall that conveniently within walking distance there is a grocery store. How long do you think you'll stay there?"

Lou and Jane looked at each other, smiled, shrugged their shoulders, and when Jane turned to Frank she said, "We haven't firmed up our plans yet, but if we decide to visit Mattituck then I suspect it'll only be for one night. Our objective is to spend most of our time at Essex."

"Good idea. Well, I enjoyed your hospitality," said Frank as he rose to leave, "and don't hesitate to shout if any other questions come to mind."

* * *

The day they left for the cruise the weather was perfect. Considering the date was set many weeks ago, they were relieved by the favorable conditions. After all, the art of predicting weather too far in advance was chancy at best, so they figured they lucked out. The early morning bright sun and cloudless sky couldn't help but bolster their excitement, and might even been viewed as a positive omen for the trip. Their boat slowly left the marina on a windless day for an extended trip under a clear blue sky, with mild temperatures which promised to warm up as the day progressed. They both wore shorts, and lightweight, water-repellant, warm jackets which would be removed as the temperature rose.

With white peaked caps, dark sunglasses, and their faces aglow with delight, they were an attractive sight. Frank waved them off with wishes for a fun-filled cruise, and thought to himself. *Ah, watching them sure stirs up memories. I shouldn't complain. What marvelous times I had. The worst part of getting old is that you know you'll never experience those glory days again. I'll just have to accept the little I can do, spend a lot of time on the boat, make do with what's possible, even take her out on the River once in a while, and drink too much at night to dispel my loneliness.*

* * *

This was a special day for Jane and Lou. Everything had fallen into place, and they eagerly looked forward to visiting new marinas, while relishing the expectation of spending a week together on the boat. All possible details had been checked and double checked: the gas tanks were filled; the engines retuned and oil levels checked; water tanks filled; food and drink supplies had been purchased and stored; clothing for all ranges of temperature and weather were organized; and the newly purchased safety harnesses (advised by Frank) were unwrapped, brought up to the bridge, and stowed in the compartment under the seat, along with the P.F.D.s (personal flotation devices). It was impossible to have imagined how grateful they would eventually be to Frank for his urging the purchase of the harnesses. Unexpectedly in the not too distant future they were to learn how valuable they were. When caught in a threatening situation, the harnesses made a considerable difference in keeping them safe and injury-free, and maybe even saved their lives.

Jane took over the helm once they reached the Sound, and was thrilled when Lou said, "This is your big day, good-looking, let's see you bring us into Greenwich. It's a kind of solo graduation . . . only I'll be right here."

"I know the *Buoys* and all the rules, so it'll be a piece of cake," boasted Jane. "But I need a little practice with the throttles. Now stand-by while I first slow us down, and then stop. That went well, so now I'll back up a bit, and then proceed ahead."

"I couldn't have done it any better," said Lou. "But for the time being, I'll take over when docking."

"Whatever you say, skipper. After all, the last thing we need is for me to crash into another boat," added Jane while enjoying her responsibility as master of the helm. "I know docking is the ultimate challenge. Probably best for me to practice on an empty dock where I can't damage anyone else."

After lunch at Greenwich, a fairly short due east trip brought them to Stamford where they stayed the night. The next morning they were awakened by the sun's cheerful rays which shone in through the open hatch above their heads.

Jane, bright-eyed and eager jumped up to begin her morning rituals, while Lou still lingered in bed a bit longer as usual. By the time they reached the open waters of the Sound it was apparent that conditions had modified. The surface of the water was now actively moving, no swells or breakers but choppy, covered with wind-blown ripples. Yesterday's calm flat surface was gone. The warm wind was gentle, with a velocity that felt no more than three-to-five-mph. It was a noteworthy change of no concern to the many recreational power boaters who found it a bit refreshing, while to the sailors it was cheerfully welcomed as they rushed to raise sails.

After nonchalantly scanning the sky, Lou commented, "You know, Jane, it takes the wind to change the weather." It was obvious he enjoyed the role of teacher, to which Jane always listened intently and soaked up information like a sponge.

She smiled to herself with the thought, *Oh how much he relishes knowing more about boating than I do, but I love him dearly and would never hurt his feelings with a heedless comment, even in jest.*

"It'll still be a warm sunny day," continued Lou, "only notice those large white cumulus clouds drifting in out of the west. As long as they remain white it won't rain and the sun will continue to shine. When they change to grey and then black, expect rain. I'm glad we put our jackets on to start the day, the wind sure is picking up."

The leisurely trip across the Sound to Mattituck, a distance of roughly 50-miles, took a few hours. There wasn't any hurry, so they traveled at a moderate pace, and didn't push it to get up on plane. If they were more attentive, as well as more knowledgeable, the minor weather changes would have signaled the approach of a Low weather front with a mix of the following: heavy cloud cover; rain of varied intensity; winds that could reach gale force; and water disruptions in the Sound that could be quite hazardous, mainly for recreational boats. The drop in the barometer—if they had one and bothered to check it—would have also alerted them that a change in the weather was coming. Even though the center of the huge Low was a long ways off out west, its outer edges had already impacted the Sound, as evidenced by the reversal of the prevailing High's clockwise wind spin to the Low's counterclockwise spin. Observant skippers quickly recognized these changes and understood they were reliable early signs of approaching unpleasant weather, and planned accordingly. The time it will take for the full force of the Low to reach the Sound is hard to estimate. Its easterly movement is largely governed by the wind's force, whose complex dynamics made predictions difficult.

Lou's attention was solely focused on the approach to and berthing at Mattituck for the night, and he looked forward to the following day's cruising across to Essex. It didn't enter his consciousness that serious disruptive weather changes might be approaching that could delay his plans.

Jane, who had the wheel, did comment, "Lou, I notice that the boat is drifting to port, and I have to continuously make steering corrections to counter it. I feel like I sort have to pull the boat back on course."

"Don't worry about it," confidently replied Lou. "Just continue with the adjustments you've been doing. Could be that it's caused by the tidal currents or the wind, or some combination of both. As long as you keep your eye on the compass and follow the Loran's updated headings we'll be fine. That amazing gadget will reliably lead us right to Mattituck. It certainly was worth every penny we paid for it."

As they neared the northern coast of Long Island, Jane called out, "We're right on target with our navigation, Lou. I can see the Deep-Draft Offshore Platform almost dead ahead. The Mattituck Inlet is just beyond it. Good for old Frank. His advice and information has been impeccable. Now I believe it's time for you to take over, skipper. To be perfectly honest, I admit I'm intimidated by the Creek itself. It looks so terribly narrow and curved, with boats of all kinds tied up along its sides, and probably has boat traffic coming down. I know that the better part of wisdom calls for a steadier hand at the helm than mine. I gladly surrender the control of the boat to you."

* * *

The following morning presented a series of telling signs of troublesome weather, which Lou either failed to appropriately respond to, or maybe he didn't recognize their significance. In hindsight, when lapses such as these are recalled, they stir bitter regrets, and are known as SHOULD HAVES.

Even before Jane and Lou got out of bed, they realized the unusual rocking of the boat and sound of the wind meant that its strength had appreciatively increased. The first SHOULD HAVE was Lou's failure to fully grasp the potential of the increased wind velocity. He also was unaware that the wind's shift to a counterclockwise spin was evidence of a significant weather change.

Lou had an additional blind spot. He simply didn't know the meaning of the flags routinely flown from the poles at dockmaster's huts. This lack of knowledge became a SHOULD HAVE casualty. Experienced skippers always kept an eye on the flags since they signaled information about the prevailing weather. If he knew about the flags, the current bright red, triangular-shaped pennant waving vigorously at Mattituck would have informed him that a Small Craft Advisory was in effect. This meant that wind speeds ranged between 25 to 38-mph, with gusts approaching Gale force level of 55-mph. A momentary glance at the flag would have told him all this, and served to warn that boating conditions were threatening.

Besides supervising the care and the operation of their marinas, dockmasters have the responsibility to monitor the weather and fly the appropriate flag. Lou's ignorance once again amounted to a SHOULD HAVE.

Despite his mastery of ship handling and docking, he was sadly lacking experience and understanding of the manifold dangers intrinsic in foul weather, especially the risk to life and vessel when boating during very extreme conditions.

Fixated on the next phase of their plans to re-cross the Sound and sail to Essex, Jane and Lou hustled through breakfast and made ready for departure. Why Lou was blind to the increasingly strong winds, and its potential to foment considerable upheaval in the waters of the Sound, was hard to understand. His stubbornness and self-confidence, with a preference to be self-taught, under other circumstances could be viewed as positive traits, but in the marine world were probably handicaps and for Lou, his 'Achilles heel.'

On Jane's part, she was a real novice who had no responsibility, and naturally relied totally on Lou. He. on the other hand, besides lacking meteorological knowledge, was also likely trying to assume a macho-bravado pose, with which to impress Jane.

Two significant events occurred just as they prepared to leave which SHOULD HAVE given him cause to hesitate, but they didn't. The first came from a woman on a boat just arriving. Her loud voice could be heard throughout the marina as she yelled, "I never before saw such awful conditions out there. It's worth your life. Thank god we safely made it in."

Despite her warning of dire conditions in the Sound, Lou elected to cast off. As the boat slowly started to move out of the slip it suddenly lunged forward. Instead of the intended throttle settings for idle-speed, the boat accelerated rapidly across the narrow watery lane, no more than 50-ft wide, towards a cruiser berthed directly ahead. A fierce gust of powerful wind had gripped the boat and literally propelled it towards a disastrous crash. To Lou's credit, he narrowly avoided the collision by immediate and prudent use of the throttles and helm. Still, this additional demonstration of the wind's awesome power was ignored—an ill-boding SHOULD HAVE.

These cautionary events SHOULD HAVE made Lou reconsider leaving. But he failed to heed the obvious. The warnings were clear, and he SHOULD HAVE stayed in the marina.

CHAPTER SIXTEEN

The dreary day had its impact. Jane and Lou both felt uncomfortable with the drop in temperature and the wind-driven heavy moisture laden air. Even a woolen sweater along with their jackets failed to keep out the dampness. The lowering stratus-type clouds covered the sky as with a grey blanket, shut out the sun, and though it wasn't raining at the moment indications were that it would before long. Overly eager to leave, Lou energetically hustled in preparation for departure and said, "Jane, let's try to get going as soon as possible. The weather tends to localize, and maybe out towards Essex we'll find some sun."

"Sure thing, love. I'll just get the breakfast things cleaned up and stowed away, and off we go," brightly replied Jane. To herself she thought, *Something has taken the edge off Lou. I noticed it last night when we walked into the village. He was quieter than usual. We bought a fine-looking New York Strip steak, about three quarters of an inch thick with just enough marbleizing to give it a scrumptious taste without being too greasy. Lou cooked it just right on our little charcoal grill, and we couldn't have eaten better. The only disappointment was our bottle of red wine. We agreed it was drinkable, but ended up feeding the fish with close to half a bottle left over.*

Lou seemed distracted, but brightened up when I suggested we turn in early so we'll be fresh for an early start. I expected when we snuggled up in bed that our nightly coupling would cheer him up, as it usually does, but somehow it didn't quite. We never missed a night embraced in heated sex, and always fell asleep with our bodies wrapped together. He didn't hold back or hesitate, but a woman can tell. He simply hadn't the fervor. Today's gloomy weather has affected him. Is he worried? Maybe not worried, but a little depressed.

After the scary start that morning, about which Lou hadn't said a word—nor did Jane ask anything—he seemed withdrawn into himself and was silent. Jane knew something had gone wrong, and tried to be upbeat. As the boat now slowly moved downstream she was comforted by her confidence in Lou's boat-handling skills. The less intense wind on the Creek—while actually caused by the shelter of bordering trees and high ground—could have been misread by Lou as a sign of improving weather.

Down near the inlet, right after the last turn, it looked like the entire fishing fleet was tied up on the west side of the Creek. They were large, weather-beaten, wooden-hulled vessels, with a prominent array of strange gear cluttering their decks. The original paint had long since faded which intensified their drab appearance. Since their primary objective was to catch fish, then improving the vessel's esthetics was clearly judged a waste of time and money. Jane couldn't resist holding her nose and said, "My, what a pungent fishy odor when the wind blows our way. I bet the fishermen never smell it."

Before Lou could respond, she turned to look towards the Inlet, and shrieked with alarm. There crashing violently against the breakwaters were towering waves—three to five-feet in heights, maybe higher—rolling in one after the other. Instinctively she moved closer to Lou, firmly grabbed him about the waist with one arm, and in a high-pitched voice declared, "Good lord, look at those monstrous waves. What are we going to do?"

Lou had slowed the boat, and after hardly a breath in which to consider the alternatives, boldly asserted, "The waves are always the worst as they contact land. Once we pass through them we'll find fairly calm water out on the Sound." It was pure wishful thinking.

With the arrival of the Low Front severe weather was evolving. The storm's awesome forces were capable of unleashing vast destruction and devastation. The wide reach of the Low extended from the waters of the Atlantic Ocean in the east, across the Sound, westward to the metropolitan area of New

York City with its suburbs, and included the lands of the many bordering States in all directions. Impossible to predict the outcome, but if luck were to prevail, then the best that could be expected was a very seriously disruptive storm with powerful winds.

Lou's statement could only be viewed as incredibly ill-informed and totally wrong. He was either foolishly naive, or temporarily somewhat delusional.

Jane tightly hung onto Lou, and found herself momentarily speechless with the rapidly unfolding prospects. Lou looked grim and determined as he gunned the engines with full throttles and unhesitatingly charged the boat into the Inlet's maelstrom.

While barely avoiding a deadly crash into the pile of rocks forming the Inlet's western jetty, their boat entered the Sound. As far as they could see huge waves were rolling one after the other out of the northeast. Lou had never encountered conditions like these, felt a spasm of fear in his gut, and gripped the wheel with all his strength. Jane's eyes bulged with terror as she held Lou as tight as possible, and with a near hysterical tremulous voice yelled above the engine's roar and the crashing waves, "Lou, we can't go on. We must turn back."

"Jane, listen to me carefully," Lou shouted through chattering teeth. "I can't turn the boat around. It's too late. We are committed. The waves are too big. If I try to turn, one of those powerful waves will surely hit us on the side of the boat and we will broach. That is, we will capsize. There is no choice but to continue across the Sound. I'm confident that we'll manage as long as I steer directly straight into each wave, and never allow them to hit us on the port or starboard."

Lou quickly understood how best to manage the waves. To safely rise over a fast moving wave breaking high in the air was to fully gun the engines as it hit. Then as the bow sunk down into the deep trough between waves, he slowed the dive by pulling back on the throttles. There was no time to think beyond steering straight, gunning up and then slowing momentarily, as the waves closely followed each other in a never-ending chain, like soldiers marching on parade.

In desperation Jane held the stainless steel railing in front with her left hand, and with her right arm pulled herself tightly against Lou. The wild gyrations of the powerful boat challenged them both to safely maintain their balance.

It didn't take Lou long to call out once again, "Jane, please follow my instructions. We need to put on the safety harnesses. I can't release the wheel for even a moment, and I don't want you to give up a safe grip. You'll have to manage on your own. Move slowly and so very cautiously. Grip the back of my jacket firmly with your left hand and then reach back into the seat for the harnesses. If needed, my left arm will be available for you to grab. Put your harness on first and connect it to the railing in front. Then help me into mine. When that is done put on your PFD and tightly fasten it. It'll help keep you warm and provide some cushioning if you fall. I'll need your help to put on mine."

It was hard to tell whether it had started raining or whether they were getting wet from the spray of the crashing waves. Regardless, their focus was to avoid an injurious fall by hanging on firmly, especially Jane. When she felt her balance failing, and was about to fall, it was the safety harness that saved her. Without it she could have been washed overboard. Despite her initial fears and near hysteria, Jane behaved stoically. The retrieval of the harnesses and the PFDs, and her relentless struggle to dress Lou into his gear while he ran the boat, had served to calm her. But above all, Lou's smile and expression of pride in her efforts meant the most, and bolstered her self-esteem. Though non-essential conversation had already ceased, they emotionally strengthened each other with their bodies tightly held together in support. Whatever fate had sent their way they were facing it bravely. Jane slowly gained mastery over her emotions and started to feel confident that they would make the crossing safely.

Lou amazed her with his steady, non-complaining, masterful control of the boat.

She admired and loved him more than ever. Progress through the never-ending turbulent waters was slow and difficult, particularly for Lou. One false move or failure to sustain the essential headway on his part could be catastrophic. His tension had to be excessive, and the physical strain was also draining. Yet, to his credit he stood tall and rigid, without rest or reprieve. Jane wished she could help, but knew their lives were in his hands. When she looked at his wet, near-frozen hands—one gripping the helm and the other grasping both throttles—she could have wept.

Attempting to plot a course to the Connecticut River and up to Essex with these conditions was unrealistic. All Lou could do was doggedly steer directly into the waves, without deviation, and worry later about locating himself on the coast. When the wind-driven rain arrived it served to further limit Lou's vision. So he leaned forward and strained to watch the angle of the next wave so he could catch it straight-on. The only redeeming feature of the storm was that there was little chance of encountering other vessels. Actually they might have been the only boat out on the Sound. All sensible skippers had anticipated the bad weather and stayed in port securely tied up, and were at home listening to the storm reports.

Eventually they approached the coast, which seemed to suddenly pop-up out of the mist and fog. Lou shouted to Jane, "Keep your eyes peeled for a *Buoy* and listen for its sound: a bell or gong. And maybe we'll spot a flashing light. I think we've drifted west of the Connecticut River. If we're lucky, that might put us outside the Clinton Harbor. I pulled in there once some time ago for a look-see and a gas refill. To my surprise, tucked back in there safely protected from the Sound is a fully equipped marina, including a fine seafood restaurant that is within easy walking distance from the boats. Sounds like my memory is still intact. I also recall that the approach to the Clinton Harbor is a Red gong *Buoy.* Let's find it and we're home free."

"Lou, the fog is lifting and I can see better," yelled Jane with excitement. "It's hard to be sure, but I hear a gong off to our left. Oops, I mean our port. And there's also a blinking light."

"I always said a man needs a younger woman, but I never thought her younger eyes and hearing would come in handy. O.K., love, hang on, we're going to bounce and tip as I steer this old tub of ours in that direction."

Gratefully, it was the right buoy. With the invaluable help of the Navigational Aids, Lou guided the boat down the long, curved approach channel into the safety and calm waters of the Clinton Marina.

EPILOGUE

Not a word was uttered. They sat together on the seat up on the bridge, with Jane's arm still holding Lou and both still wearing their harnesses and PFDs. They were drained, green with exhaustion, weak from hunger and thirst, and physically and emotionally so depleted that it was completely impossible, at the moment, to fathom how they incredibly managed to avoid disaster, nor could they muster the strength to celebrate.

With a welcoming smile the Dockmaster offered them a slip for the night. He was an old salt, looked like he'd been around boats and boaters for most of his life, and had a quiet congenial manner. Without asking any questions, he recognized the residual look of fear in their eyes and the washed-out appearance of sailors who had gone through a terrible experience. Furthermore, he added, "I'm putting you in the visitors slip. Don't worry about a thing. It's yours until the storm blows out and you can resume your cruise. I suspect the worst will pass through tonight, and by tomorrow I wouldn't be surprised to see a little sun. It's been a long hard day for you, so rest up, but keep in mind that the restaurant won't need a reservation, but they start closing up by nine."

They peeled off their damp, soiled clothes, crawled into bed, reached for each other, hugged, kissed, immediately fell asleep—and for the first time without a sexual nightcap. During the night the storm raged with thunder and lightning, while the high winds forcibly rocked the boat. Jane and Lou slept so deeply that even the worst of the storm's tumult didn't disturb them. They had reached the end of an ability to care or worry, and their totally wasted minds and bodies craved oblivion.

* * *

As the old guy had predicted, the next day brought a clearing sky with the wind reduced to a gentle breeze. By late morning Jane stirred and was surprised not to find Lou besides her. She found him sitting at the table nursing a cup of black coffee, looking off into the distance with a melancholy demeanor. Jane eased onto a seat opposite, forced a smile, and said, "You look here, skipper, you know the rules, you run the boat and I do breakfast." She paused, and without a response, continued. "Lou, dear, what's up? You can't shut down and stew inside. Get it out and we'll both together deal with it."

He looked at her and said, "I can't believe I was so stupid as to race the boat into those waves. I should have stopped, turned the boat around and went back up to Mattituck. Worst of all I needlessly put you at risk while scaring you near to death. Can you ever forgive me?"

Jane looked across at him. Reached out and grabbed his hand and squeezed tight. Then she got up, walked around the table, sat next to him, and pulled him to her in a loving embrace. For a moment he remained limp, but then placed his arms around her, buried his head in her breasts and began to sob. Tears spilled down her face as she gently stroked his head and murmured, "Love of my life, just let it flow. If it weren't for your brave skilled handling of the boat, we wouldn't have made it to safety. Your strength and iron determination were incredible. It was an awesome experience that we shared, and has added a precious bond to our relationship. Like comrades in war, we are linked with rare memories of how we both faced fear and still functioned in mutual support. I'll remember yesterday forever as special and private"

Lou stopped crying, sat up and kissed her. Jane soon pushed him back, smiled and said, "O.K. lover boy, save your passion for later. It's time for me to make breakfast."

Before they left, Lou filled the gas tanks, and they both bid farewell to the Dockmaster. Lou particularly thanked him for providing a welcome port in a storm, and promised to return for a visit. As the sun tried to break through they cruised east for the Connecticut River and then up to Essex as planned, where they enjoyed a delightful few days. The Essex Island Dockmaster surprised them on arrival when he said he took the liberty to move their reservation at the Griswold up one day because of the storm.

~ * ~ * ~

Meet our Author
Dr. Howard S. Selden, DDS

As manager of his high school football team, Howard was able to exhibit his enthusiasm for helping the injured and the sick as the age of soft leather helmets without face or mouth guards led to many displaced and broken teeth. His pursuit of medical interest led him through school and into the U. S. Army as a Dentist.

A true anecdote from his army times:

"The setting is the height of the "cold war." The defense appropriations were lopsidedly going to SAC, with their nuclear-armed bombers. At my dental facilities at Fort Riley, KS we were unable to meet our supply needs for basic dental materials. I heard that replacement parts for army vehicles, including tanks and trucks, and ammunition were also hard to get.

When I visited a friend and classmate at his SAC base, I was stunned at the overabundance of dental supplies. There was so much that it literally filled a small warehouse. You can imagine what evolved. I made periodic visits, loading my car each time with everything basic plus the newest technical do-dads. Back at Riley, I made the rounds distributing the rare goodies. My standard reply to questions (especially from my Colonel—an old-timer whose dental acumen plateaued somewhere around WWI) about where I got the stuff was to say, "It is best not to know, but you could think of it as a gift from on high."

Howard's career as a practicing Dental specialist led him into teaching and writing. He is the author of over thirty scientific papers published in Dentistry's Journal of Endodontics. He is a former Clinical Assistant Professor, Department of Endodontology, Temple University School of Dentistry, Philadelphia, PA; helped establish Dental departments in local hospitals to care for the indigent; and served as Director of the Dental Department at the Muhlenberg Hospital Center, Bethlehem, PA.

Long a fan of science fiction, his first published book was of that genre, *The Pariah Stigma*. His long-term interest in history led him into the study of ancient history and the struggle for survival by the Jewish people captured his attention with the result that three novels on a sweeping canvas from biblical to very contemporary times were generated: *An Unusual Encounter*, *The Shaman and The Jew* and *Wapasha and the Jew.*

Howard and his wife Tamara reside in Pennsylvania, close to the ski slopes, where his three children often joined him and Tamara for winter fun-time.

www.ingramcontent.com/pod-product-compliance
Lightning Source LLC
Chambersburg PA
CBHW070109030726
47506CB00002B/663
9781942981190